He leaned toward her again, running the back of his index finger along her cheekbone, watching, giving her a chance to pull away, but she wasn't pulling away.

She was leaning into his touch, her eyes hazing over, her lips parting.

A voice in his head was saying no, was saying that he was crossing the very line he'd told himself he couldn't cross, but it was a small voice, close to noiseless, and then it was gone.

He looked at her lips, and then he moved in, taking them slowly, tasting cognac and warmth, feeling his pulse heating, gathering.

And then her mouth was softening, molding to his.

She was kissing him back, pulling him closer, and suddenly he was free-falling, hungrier for her than he'd ever felt for anyone.

He cupped her nape, deepening the kiss, exploring the sweet wet heat in her mouth, feeling desire blazing through his veins, feeling her hands in his hair, tugging him closer, deeper and deeper...

Dear Reader,

I'm so excited to bring you my first ever Christmas romance for Harlequin! Set in Paris and Chamonix, this is a story I've been wanting to write for a while, ever since I learned about extreme freeriding (via a friend whose son-in-law is a famous world-class freerider).

For extreme athletes, issues around relationships and family can be thorny and complex. How much risk is too much? How can family fit into an extreme sports lifestyle?

I've never been on a snowboard, but I've had a blast researching this story. I'm particularly indebted to all the extreme snowboarders out there who post inspiring (and heart-stopping) videos on social media. I literally could not have written this story without them.

I hope you enjoy reading *The Single Dad's Christmas Proposal* as much as I enjoyed writing it!

Ella x

The Single Dad's Christmas Proposal

Ella Hayes

———

HARLEQUIN

Romance

HARLEQUIN®
Romance™

Recycling programs for this product may not exist in your area.

ISBN-13: 978-1-335-40686-6

The Single Dad's Christmas Proposal

Copyright © 2021 by Ella Hayes

All rights reserved. No part of this book may be used or reproduced in any manner whatsoever without written permission except in the case of brief quotations embodied in critical articles and reviews.

This is a work of fiction. Names, characters, places and incidents are either the product of the author's imagination or are used fictitiously. Any resemblance to actual persons, living or dead, businesses, companies, events or locales is entirely coincidental.

This edition published by arrangement with Harlequin Books S.A.

For questions and comments about the quality of this book, please contact us at CustomerService@Harlequin.com.

Harlequin Enterprises ULC
22 Adelaide St. West, 40th Floor
Toronto, Ontario M5H 4E3, Canada
www.Harlequin.com

Printed in U.S.A.

After ten years as a television camerawoman, **Ella Hayes** started her own photography business so that she could work around the demands of her young family. As an award-winning wedding photographer, she's documented hundreds of love stories in beautiful locations, both at home and abroad. She lives in central Scotland with her husband and two grown-up sons. She loves reading, traveling with her camera, running and great coffee.

Books by Ella Hayes

Harlequin Romance

Her Brooding Scottish Heir
Italian Summer with the Single Dad
Unlocking the Tycoon's Heart
Tycoon's Unexpected Caribbean Fling

Visit the Author Profile page at Harlequin.com.

For my brother, Steven, and all the other
fearless ones...

PROLOGUE

Chamonix, December 5th...

'YOU'RE OFTEN DESCRIBED as fearless. Are you?'

Dax D'Aureval felt a string of nerves tightening in his ribs. Was the microphone clipped to his jacket picking up the quick beats of his heart? He could feel his blood rushing, pounding in his ears. He drew a slow breath, allowing the familiar feelings to settle, then he looked past the camera lens and into Pierre's expectant face. 'Really? You're asking me this again?'

Pierre's nod was slight, but his eyes held a gleam.

Dax let out a slow sigh. Pierre filmed all his snowboarding exploits for the sponsors, but for the documentary features action shots alone weren't enough. They needed interview material to use as voice-over, talking head stuff because his fans liked to see his face. The whites of his eyes! They wanted to know what made him tick. As if he even knew! All he could ever do was answer Pierre's questions, in whichever moment they came, as honestly as he could, dialling up the charm, of course. He had over a hundred and seventy thousand followers on social media and his job was to keep the brands he represented in the spotlight. If that meant schmoozing to camera, coming out with little quips that could be used as teasers for the documentaries, then that was fine. It was part of the sponsorship gig, part of the life he'd created for himself. Free riding was his passion so talking about it wasn't a hardship, except that at that moment his insides were chaos, and his throat was dry. He was about to take on a Chamonix classic—the Mallory Couloir on the north face of the Aiguille du Midi—and what he needed was to be taking a moment, sifting through his fear, sorting it into good and bad, not answering questions about it.

He flicked a glance at the lift. His support team was hovering by the doors, waiting for him. His guides. His friends. *Crazy steep-skiing machines!* They all spent their lives romancing the slopes. He wasn't the only one.

He took a breath, strapping on his game face. 'I wouldn't describe myself as fearless... Not at all. You can't do what I do and not be scared.' He swallowed. 'Like right now I'm really scared, but I don't try to block my fear because it's useful, even if it's annoying.' He smiled, principally to loosen the tightness in his cheeks. 'Fear primes you for danger. It keeps you on your toes. It's a strange fear, though...' A tingle moved along his spine. 'I kind of love it.'

The camera moved closer. 'Love is a strong word, Dax, but is it love, or could it be an addiction?'

He could see his own reflection in the lens, could see the intent in Pierre's eyes. Yes, the lines he rode looked reckless... Yes, it might have seemed to a casual observer that he was in the grip of a dangerous addiction, that he was a man who liked flirting with death, but free riding was about living not dying, and Pierre got that because Pierre was an extreme snowboarder too. Pierre was only prodding him because he was on a crusade to debunk the myth that extreme sports were the domain of cavalier, thrill-seeking adrenaline junkies. Usually he fell in, but today, for some reason, he didn't want to. Maybe it was because the lens was too close, or because the guys by the lift were getting restive, or maybe it was because his stomach was gnawing a hole in itself. He could feel himself sliding into the *Why the hell am I doing this?* headspace and he had to shake it off before it took hold. He needed to get onto the mountain, face his fear, find the beauty on the other side of it.

He shifted slightly. 'I don't know if it's an addiction…but it *is* an obsession.' He paused. 'When I'm riding there's a spirit inside me that *is* wild, definitely a little crazy…' He could sense Pierre stiffening, but he was invested now. He had to keep going. 'I don't understand it, but it drives me, keeps me wanting more. Higher. Harder. Faster. I'm always chasing something…' He shrugged, holding in a smile. 'Is that addiction?'

'Dax!' The camera tilted in Pierre's hand. 'That's the wrong answer.'

He felt a pang of guilt. 'I'm sorry, man. It's all I've got today.' His veins were thrumming, chemicals flooding in, preparing him for what he was about to do. He unclipped the microphone, handing it back to Pierre, then he picked up his pack. 'You should use it anyway because it's the truth, even if you don't want to hear it.' His insides were boiling, turning to liquid. 'I mean, yes, we plan for risk. We've got the experience, the skills, the equipment. We take every precaution, but there's no denying it: we seek out impossible lines, lines that have never been ridden before and we ride them hard.' He shrugged. 'It follows that we must be a little bit crazy.'

CHAPTER ONE

Paris, December 5th, one year later...

SIMONE COSSART HURRIED across the Place du Palais Royal, squinting through the spiralling snowflakes, resisting the urge to lift her face and catch some on her tongue. She loved snow, the way it transformed the city into a wonderland, but dallying wasn't an option. She wanted to get to the bistro first, ahead of Dax D'Aureval, so she could seem calm and collected when he arrived, 'seem' being the operative word, since she wasn't feeling remotely calm.

Maybe she was mad, bending over backwards to meet Dax at such short notice. It wasn't as if he'd ever bent over backwards for her. He'd never been to pick up his son, Yannick, from her apartment, and he'd never reciprocated a play-date for her daughter, Chloe, even though Chloe and Yann had been best friends from their first day in Cours Préparatoire. It was always Amy,

Dax's au pair, who came to collect Yannick. It was Amy who'd warned her quietly before Yann and Chloe's first playdate that Yann's *maman* was dead and that she shouldn't ask Yann about her. Amy hadn't elaborated, and at the time Simone had been too preoccupied with her new job in the school's office—her first proper job in years—to give it much thought. She'd simply been glad that Chloe was settling in at school and had made such a nice friend, but now all the things she didn't know about Yann and his mysterious *papa* were weighing heavy. She was flying blind, meeting Dax to discuss a business proposal because Amy had asked her to, but she didn't quite know what to make of it!

She dipped her chin, bracing herself against the swirl. Why hadn't she brought a hat? Gloves? She'd seen the forecast! It was why she'd made sure that Chloe had been well wrapped up that morning but, somehow, she'd forgotten to wrap herself up and now she was paying the price. Her fingers were freezing, her nose was probably red, and she could feel snow settling in her hair and melting wetly on her cheeks. Calm and collected? *Not!*

She marched on, head down, until she reached the corner of the square and then she stopped. This was the place! Bistro Royal. Crimson canopies edged with twinkling lights, windows lushly decked with Christmas greenery, glowing interior. *Lovely!* She stood, staring, feeling nostalgic. This was what she'd come to Paris for a decade ago, to be a part of this…this city of lights and romance, this city of lively cafés and big dreams…

Broken dreams…

She bit her lips together. No point dwelling on that. There were more pressing things to think about, like getting inside, drying off and making herself presentable!

She hurried towards the entrance, brushing snow off her coat, going for the door handle just as a gloved male hand claimed it.

'Oh—' She drilled her toes hard into the paving, slewing to a halt, but somehow she was still moving, pitching forwards.

'Whoa!' A firm hand closed around her arm, holding it fast. 'God, I'm sorry! Are you all right?'

At the pulsing edge of her vision, she perceived a blue jacket. She touched her chest, catching her breath. 'Yes, I think so.'

'Are you sure?' He was letting go of her arm, stepping back.

'Yes, I'm fine, really, and it wasn't your fault…' She gathered herself, looking up. 'I was rush—' Her tongue stuck. Monsieur Blue Jacket was devilishly handsome, and curiously familiar, the bit of him she could see anyway between the band of his dark green beanie and the turned-up collar of his jacket. He was clean-shaven, dark browed, and his large brown eyes were flecked with mischief, or maybe it was the canopy lights that were making them twinkle all the way to their warm seductive depths. It was hard to tell, hard to breathe.

A slow smile dented his cheeks. 'I was rushing too, to get out of the snow—' he closed one eye, scrunching his face a little '—which is weird because actually I love snow.'

'Me too…although…' He was dragging off the hat, releasing a dark mop of supremely touchable hair. She curled her fingers into her palms, 'Although I wish I hadn't forgotten *my* hat.'

'Here!' His hand shot out, dangling the beanie. 'Take mine.'

She felt her mouth falling open. Was he for real? Who offered their hat to a total stranger just like that? Her heart thumped. Was he hitting on her? *Oh, God!* She swallowed hard. 'It's extremely kind of you but I couldn't possibly—'

'Yes, you can. I want you to have it.' He dipped his chin, eyes half teasing, half serious. 'I have an endless supply of hats so I can definitely spare this one for a lady in need.'

Her heart pulsed. In need didn't come close!

She was burning up with it, tingling from head to toe, and it was clear from the look in his eyes that he could see it, knew exactly what effect he was having on her. He was playing, flirting, and suddenly she realised that she didn't mind one little bit. She liked him, liked the way his eyes were travelling over her face, lingering on her mouth, then moving up and reaching into hers again. She could feel her body responding, liquid warmth spreading through her limbs. If she accepted his hat, would something happen? Maybe the hat was a sign…

Stop!

She broke away from his gaze. What was she doing, weaving silly fantasies? She wasn't looking for a man, and as for serendipity and dreams coming true, she didn't believe in all that. Not any more. She shivered, feeling cold. Her dreams had all been trampled. She'd lost her love and, with him, her rose-tinted view of the world. That was all this silly flirtation was. A rose-tinted moment, briefly warm.

'Go on…' His voice pulled her back. He was brushing off the hat, scattering drops, his eyes twinkling. 'Think of it as compensation for almost knocking you over.'

'You didn't! It was me, not looking where…'

His eyebrows slid upwards.

She felt the air softening, a sudden warmth

filling her chest. He seemed determined to give her his hat and the light in his eyes was making it impossible to refuse. She pressed her lips together then reached out, smiling. 'Okay. Thank you! It'll make my walk back to the Metro much warmer.' She tucked it into her pocket. 'You're very chivalrous.'

A smile touched his lips. 'I don't know about that but, thank you.' His eyes held hers for a beat, and then he blinked. 'I should probably go inside. I'm meeting someone.'

A gorgeous girlfriend no doubt! She nipped off the thought with a smile. 'Me too.'

He yanked the door open, standing back, and then she felt the briefest light touch between her shoulder blades. 'After you.'

In the ladies' room she set her bag down, waiting for the ghost of his touch to fade, and then she looked in the mirror.

Oh, God! She was a mess, all damp and smudged. Still, she could fix her face and hair. Fixing the chaos she was feeling inside was a different matter. How could a fleeting encounter at the door have put her into such a spin?

She went to unzip her bag, then stopped, reaching into her pocket for the hat. Cashmere soft. She flipped the label. *Wow!* Actually cashmere! She lifted it to her face, breathing in his smell. *Clean!* He'd smell good, close up, she knew it. Fresh…like mountain air. *Yes!* He had that outdoorsy glow, the traces of a summer tan, oh, and those melting eyes, the unhurried way he'd looked at every part of her face… A tingle played along her spine and she hugged it tight. *Feeling!* How long had it been since she'd felt so aware of someone, so trembly and dizzy in all the right ways? Kaboom! He'd woken her up, just by looking at her.

She let her hands fall. Men didn't usually look at her like that, or maybe she just didn't notice them because André was always there, even though he was gone. No one's smile had ever matched his. No one's gaze had ever stopped her heart the way his used to. She'd kept his flame burning for Chloe, so that Chloe would know how deeply her *papa* had loved her, and for herself, because memories were all she had left. They'd kept her going through the silent weeping days, and the ranting inside days, and the day that his parents had turned their backs. She squeezed her eyes shut, pushing the thought out of reach. For the past three years all she'd thought about was making Chloe happy, and making ends meet, but now a stranger's gaze had stolen her breath away and her senses were ringing like Christmas bells, ringing for *herself.*

The door sprang open and she startled, stuffing the beanie back into her pocket. The girl coming in was beautiful, powdering the air with her instantly recognisable fragrance: two hundred euros a bottle! Was *she* the one he was meeting? They'd look good together...

Stop!

She slipped off her coat and dug out her hairbrush, working it upwards through her damp tangles. Why was she poking at jealous little fires? Didn't she have enough to poke at already: a hastily arranged meeting; an offer from a man she'd never even met? That was what she needed to be thinking about, even though it still didn't feel real...

Amy had come to the school office that morning ashen-faced. Her father had just been diagnosed with myeloma, she said. The prognosis was bad. She was going back to Melbourne just as soon as Dax could find her a flight. Simone had still been processing that news when Amy had dropped another bomb. Would *she* consider stepping in to help Dax look after Yannick over Christmas at his chalet in Chamonix? She'd asked the obvious question: wasn't there a relative who could help, or a childminder in Chamonix? Amy had said, no, it was complicated. She'd said Dax would explain everything if Simone agreed to meet him, and then she'd said he'd pay her whatever she wanted if she agreed to go. A well-aimed strike! Amy knew she was hard up. Amy knew that Chloe was only at Yann's expensive private school because of her job in the school office, and Amy had seen her apartment in all its miserable glory: the peeling paint, the torn kitchen lino. Amy had heard the incessant dripping of the kitchen tap.

She wound her hair up catching it with an elastic. Amy knew she hated the apartment, knew that she was planning to move as soon as she passed her probation period at the school and could count on her salary. In short, Amy knew that a cash injection would make a world of difference.

There! Her hair was done. She dampened a tissue, cleaning the mascara smudges from around her eyes. Getting paid to spend Christmas in Chamonix definitely wasn't a horrible idea, although her parents would be disappointed if she and Chloe didn't go to the farm. She breathed through a stab of the usual guilt. Maman and Papa didn't know how things had been for her since André's death, how strapped for cash she'd been. Telling them would only have led to questions that were too painful to answer and she wasn't ready, wouldn't be until she was properly on her feet again. She took out her lipstick and dabbed some on. But that day was coming—soon—and then she'd be able to let them in again. In the meantime, if she agreed to go to Chamonix, she wouldn't mention the money. She'd say it was an invitation she couldn't turn down for Chloe's sake. At least that part would be true!

She popped her lipstick away and zipped up her bag. The money was a magnet, but even without it the chance to give Chloe a magical Christmas in the mountains would have been tempting. Chloe loved snow, loved making snow bunnies. Wonky ears. Twigs for whiskers! Simone felt a smile coming. And 'chalet' sounded so cosy. She could see it in her mind, crackling fires, and fur throws. All the clichés! And even though Christmas was her worst time of year because of André, being somewhere different—somewhere where she wasn't having to dodge Maman's unsubtle attempts to fix her up with a lonely farmer—would maybe make things easier. And Yann wasn't hard work! He was deeply quiet, but he seemed to adore Chloe and Chloe adored him right back. No wonder! He was cute as, with his big eyes, and his dark eyebrows and his dark mop of curly hair…

Her heart pulsed. *No!* She gripped the sink unit, replaying the scene at the door. That feeling of familiarity. The shape of his nose, his mouth, his hair springing free… *Oh, God!* How hadn't she seen it straight away? Monsieur Blue

Jacket was the spit of Yannick. The man who'd set her senses alight was Dax D'Aureval!

Dax glanced at the entrance, then scanned the interior yet again. Simone Cossart was due to arrive at any moment—skinny, according to Amy, with serious eyes and dark hair—but he couldn't stop perusing the tables, looking for the woman he'd almost knocked over at the door.

He'd been head down, churning away over Amy's sad news, feeling sorry for her, and—*yes*—feeling sorry for himself, and then somehow, she'd been there, his very own snow angel with snowflakes melting on her cheeks and nestling in her hair like confetti. For a few heavenly moments, her warm eyes and lovely smile had sent his spirits skywards. For the first time in months he'd felt alive, but now she was nowhere to be seen and he wanted to see her. A glimpse would do, from a distance, just something… anything…anything at all.

Stop!

This wasn't him, tangling himself up in the thought of someone. He never did this, ever! He squeezed his eyes shut. Maybe it was just another symptom of his disarray. His life was out of control, so why not his emotions too? That would be the cherry on top! He slumped back in his chair, feeling a drag of weariness.

Was he really here, in a Parisian bistro, trying to solve a childcare emergency? Four months ago he hadn't even been a father, hadn't had an unfathomable six-year-old son who froze him out at every opportunity. Four months ago he'd been free as a bird, packing his gear for a new free-riding adventure in Alaska—

'Hello...'

His heart pulsed. *Snow Angel?* Grey dress, tidy hair, red lips. Different from before yet the same.

'You're Dax D'Aureval, aren't you?' She was looking at him carefully, blushing slightly. 'Yannick's *papa*?'

'Yes, but...' He blinked, trying to clear the confusion in his head, then he looked at her again. Dark hair. *Like Amy said.* Serious eyes. *Like Amy said.* For a beat, the room stood still, then a small spark of joy ignited deep in his chest. '*You're* Simone Cossart?'

She nodded. 'Yes.'

'Wow!' *What?* He shot to his feet, heart racing. 'I mean, hello, again!'

'Hi... Again!' A smile lit her gaze, but there was wariness behind it. Was she already planning her escape? *Hell's bells!* If he'd known who she was, he'd never have flirted with her at the door. He felt a fluttering panic. Too late to rewind, but he could hit the reset button, make her see that this was business, pure and simple. He *had* to get her on board. Yann's happiness and his own career depended on it.

'So...' He moved round the table, pulling out a chair for her, keeping his tone light. 'That was funny, us meeting like that. Not knowing...'

'Very!' Her eyes caught his, holding him as he sat down again. 'The thing is, I actually thought there was something familiar about you.' She was smiling now, wariness fading. He felt a wash of relief. Dealing with it up front had been the right call. 'I can't believe I didn't see it right away. I mean, Yannick is the spit of you!'

It was exactly what he'd thought when Yann's picture had pinged onto his phone. No DNA test required! He forced out a smile. 'Yes, he is, although his eyes are lighter.'

Like Zara's. He felt a lick of anger. It was wrong, thinking ill of the dead, but he couldn't not be furious with Zara. She should have told him he had a son. She'd known he was a D'Aureval, but, aside from his family's wealth and status, at twenty-two he'd been a public figure in his own right, a rising star on the world free-riding circuit. She could have contacted him so easily, but instead she'd kept Yann to herself, and now *he* was dealing with the fallout, messing up constantly, and that wasn't his style. Christ, if he'd been in the habit of messing up—

'Are you ready to order?'

Somehow a waitress was there, looking at him. He shook himself. 'Simone? What would you like?'

Simone smiled at the girl. '*Café au lait*, and a glass of water, please.'

'And for you, *monsieur*?'

'I'll take an espresso, thanks. That's all.'

The girl tapped at a device in her hand, and then she was gone.

He looked at Simone. 'So, we should probably start. Amy said you can't stay long…?'

'That's right.' She smiled apologetically. 'Chloe's at ballet. I have to collect her.'

'Okay.' He smiled to hide his nerves. He wasn't used to divulging information about his private life, but it was the only way. He had to make her see that she was the only one who could help him. He took a breath. 'So thanks for coming. Obviously, you know that Amy's leaving…'

'Yes.' Her eyelids fluttered. 'It's so awful about her father.' She shook her head a little. 'Why do bad things always seem to happen at Christmas?'

Had she been through something herself? It seemed as though maybe she had, but now wasn't the time to ask. He shrugged. 'I don't know, but it's terrible for her and, frankly, for me as well. She's been a big help.' Connecting with Yann in a way that he couldn't, in a way that he didn't even seem to be equipped for. He pushed the thought away, trying to sound upbeat. 'It was her idea to ask you, you know. She says you're good with Yannick.'

'Well…' She seemed to falter. 'Yann's easy…'

Easy? He felt an ache in his chest. Yann was quiet but there was nothing easy about him, not for *him* anyway.

Her eyebrows flickered. 'Most of the time I hardly know he's there.'

'There' being her apartment, a place he'd made a point of avoiding. His stomach churned. He might have planned a careful route into this conversation, but the guilt he was feeling about Yann's frequent playdates with Chloe was all too real, especially now that Simone was sitting right there in front of him.

'Simone…' It was hard to hold her gaze. 'Thanks for having Yann over so often.' He took a breath. 'I'm sorry we haven't reciprocated yet.'

She blinked. 'It's okay.'

'It isn't—' He could see a splinter of hurt in her eyes, could feel it piercing his own skin. 'You've been kind and I've been rude. I didn't mean to be. It's just that…'

'Just that what?'

He felt despair winding through his veins.

'I'm useless at the whole parenting thing, okay! Meeting other parents. Talking to them. Play-dates!' He held her gaze, loading his voice so she would understand. 'It's all new to me.'

'New?' Her eyebrows drew in. 'But Yann's six.'

'Yes…but you see, he was with his mother—'

'Café au lait?'

He leant back, giving the waitress space, taking the moment to breathe. He'd got to base camp, but his nerves were fraying. Opening up wasn't his thing. Hiding behind a cut-out was his thing. Cut-out Dax was a thrill-seeker, a playboy. Cut-out Dax was always smiling, always upbeat. But Yann's arrival had turned him over, reminded him of what was on his flip side, and now, for Yann's sake, he needed to lay himself out for Simone, like cards on a table. No wonder his mouth was dry.

He took a sip of his coffee, steeling himself. 'Simone, Yannick only came to me four months ago, after his mother died. Before that, I didn't even know he existed.'

Her eyes flew wide. 'His *maman* only died four months ago?' And then the second thing he'd said seemed to find fertile ground. 'You didn't know about him?' Her mouth was hanging open just as his had been when Zara's father, Claude, had called, but he'd dropped his phone too, smashing the screen so that he'd had to peer through a web of cracks to see the picture of Yann that Claude texted through.

'No.' He swallowed hard, reining in his emotions. 'I had no idea. Zara and I weren't together. We had a fling. She never contacted me, never told her parents that I was Yann's father. Her *papa* found my name in her diary after she died.'

She was shaking her head. 'I don't know what to say.'

'You don't have to say anything. I'm just trying to explain why I'm struggling with the parent stuff.' The empathy in her eyes was tearing at something inside him. He sipped his coffee again, steadying himself. 'It was a shock, obviously, but after I'd come to my first thought was that I wanted to be a good parent…' Better than his mother, Colette, better than his anonymous, absent father. Admittedly, between them they'd set a low bar, giving him no template for exactly *how* to be a good parent! He pushed the thought away. 'I thought I'd have time to work things out, but Zara's parents had other ideas. They said they were too old to be running around after Yann…' Simone's eyes narrowed. She was doing the maths, but she didn't have the right figures. He sighed. 'Look, Zara was a lot older than me, and she'd been a late baby herself. Her parents are in their seventies, so fair enough. They love Yann, but they said

his place was with me. They asked me to fetch
him straight away.'

Simone was frowning. 'But that's—'

'I know.' At least they were on the same page!
'It seemed wrong to me too, but I was the absent
father without a leg to stand on, so off I went
to fetch him. No easing in. No getting to know
each other.' He felt an ache in his chest, a sag-
ging weariness. 'It's been a disaster.'

'No wonder.' She was shaking her head again.
'Yann's grieving. Displaced. And, yes, you're
his *papa*, but you're still a stranger.' She looked
down, toying with her cup, and then her eyes
were on his again, her gaze searching. 'I wish
I'd known Yann's loss was so recent. Why didn't
Amy fill me in properly?'

He felt his heart shrivelling. 'Because I asked
her not to. Yann's in a new place with new people. I thought not hearing Zara's name would
make it easier for him to settle.' Something that
looked like disagreement momentarily surfaced in her eyes but then it faded. He sighed.
'It seemed wise at the time, but probably wasn't,
I don't know...'

For a long moment she was quiet, and then
she sighed. 'I can see it's been difficult—'

'Difficult?' He felt something snap inside,
and suddenly unrehearsed words were rising on
his tongue and spilling out. 'Yann has no time

for me, Simone. I can't reach him, can't seem to make him happy no matter what I do, and I don't like other parents and other kids seeing the way he ignores me.' Was he sounding pathetic, self-pitying? Probably, but she needed to know. 'It's why I don't do playdates, why I've never been to collect him from your apartment.'

'But that's—'

'Stupid?' He gulped a breath. 'Pathetic?'

'No.' Her eyes were filling, glistening. 'I was going to say, it's understandable.'

His throat went tight. She really was an angel, a kind, sweet, beautiful angel. Talking to her, confiding in her, was beginning to feel like a sweet release. He took a breath. 'I'm not used to failing, but I'm failing with Yann. I can't seem to connect with him. I don't know how. It's why I took Amy on, why I leave everything to her. Yann prefers her to me.' He closed his eyes for a beat. Final push! 'But now she's going, and I don't know what to do. It's our first Christmas together! I want Yann to be happy. If you and Chloe come with us to Chamonix then there's a good chance he will be, because Yann adores Chloe.'

Warm light filled her eyes. 'And she adores him right back, believe me.'

He felt his spirits lifting, hope kindling in his chest. 'He's fond of you too, Simone. That's

what Amy says, so, you see, it has to be you…
You, and Chloe. Yann isn't close to anyone else.'
He rested his forearms on the table and leaned
towards her, putting everything into his gaze.
'Please come with us to Chamonix, Simone.
I'll make it worth your while, pay you what-
ever you want…'

Whatever I want…

Dax's gaze was intense, full of hope, too hard
to hold. She looked down, staring past the skin
on her untouched coffee. Talk about releasing
the motherload. It was almost too much to process…an accidental father struggling to bond
with a grieving son, losing his trusted au pair
and turning to her, because of her daughter.
Didn't he have family who could help? Presum-
ably not, since he hadn't mentioned them. *Think!*
If she and Chloe were to go, then maybe Yann
would be happy, but would that really help Dax
in the end? If he kept stepping back, using other
people as intermediaries, he was never going to
build a bridge to his son and he clearly wanted
to. The money was a big, shiny magnet but taking it would prick her conscience if she didn't at
least try to point him in the right direction first.

She took a breath and looked up. 'Dax, I'm
not trying to talk myself out of a job or anything, but do you *really* need us?' His gaze flick-

ered. 'I mean, wouldn't Christmas be the perfect time for you and Yann to be together, just the two of you, bonding?'

'Ah!' He sat back a little, looking sheepish. 'Sorry! I should have explained before. I have to work over Christmas. The hours are erratic, so I can't be with Yann all the time.'

'I see.' Now it made sense. This wasn't just about helping him with Yannick for the Christmas holidays. He needed an actual childminder. That was better in a way. More defined. She refocused. 'So what do you do?'

He took a breath. 'I snowboard, professionally.'

That made sense too. It explained his outdoorsy glow, the athleticism that seemed to underpin his every movement. It explained the chalet in Chamonix. She felt her shoulders inching upwards. 'Are you an instructor?'

'No.' A smile broke over his face, filling his eyes with twinkling light. 'I'm a free rider.'

'Right.' He clearly loved being a free rider, whatever that was. It had brought his smile back just like that. She felt her own lips curving up. 'And what do free riders do?'

'They find their own lines.'

'Lines?' She pulled the bug-eyed face that always made Chloe laugh.

He chuckled. 'Basically, we ride outside the resorts.'

'Okay…' She picked up her glass and took a sip of water. 'I love snow, but, as you can probably tell, I know nothing about winter sports. I know ice-skating, and skiing, oh, and luge, and I only remember luge because I saw it on television once and it looked terrifying.'

His eyebrows flickered. 'Terrifying, huh?'

Was he flirting again or was it just that she was involuntarily susceptible to the light in his eyes? She put her glass down. 'So, how does free riding qualify as work? I mean, it doesn't sound much like work.'

He laughed roundly. 'I can see how you'd think that, but actually it's quite involved. There's a lot of planning, and waiting for the right conditions.'

'And you get *paid*—' She bit her tongue, felt a blush tingling in her cheeks. 'I'm sorry. It's none of my business.'

'Don't be.' His hand covered hers for a warm second, his gaze deep and kind. 'I don't mind.' She felt her lungs emptying out, warmth rushing through her veins, and then his hand was back on the table and he was smiling as if he hadn't just stopped her heart. 'I do get paid, yes. I have sponsors, brands to promote. I'm what they call an influencer. It's why I have to go to Cham.' A shadow crossed his face. 'Since Yann came, I haven't been pulling my weight for my sponsors! I need to get back to it, honour my commitments. I'm planning a big expedition.'

The set of his jaw spoke volumes. The life he loved had been ripped away and he wanted it back. She knew how that felt.

His gaze sharpened suddenly. 'You know, if you want to see what I do, you could watch one of my films.'

She felt her mouth falling open. 'You're a film star?'

'No...' His eyebrows flickered. 'But they make films about me.'

Intriguing! 'Then you must be good?'

'I'm not bad.' There was mischief in his eyes, and something else that was making her heart flutter.

She looked away, catching the time on her watch. *Oh, God!* She sprang to her feet, grabbing her bag. 'I'm sorry. I've got to go—'

'But what about Cham?' He was getting up, chair scraping. 'We haven't finished...'

He looked strained, anxious, but all she could think was that she was going to be late for Chloe, and she was never late for Chloe.

She licked her lips. 'Look, I'm leaning towards yes, but I need to think about it a bit more.'

'Okay.' And then he blinked. 'I mean, of course.' He plucked a card from his shirt pocket and handed it to her. 'Here's my number. If you have any questions, please call.'

'I will.'

And then he was moving round the table towards her, leaning in, kissing each of her cheeks in turn, making her head spin. When he stepped back his eyes were full of warm light. 'Thank you for coming.'

She smiled, suddenly remembering. 'And thank *you* for the hat.'

His face lit up. 'You're more than welcome. Hopefully, I'll see you wearing it in Chamonix…'

She bit her lip, tangling inside. 'Hopefully.'

CHAPTER TWO

December 5th, later...

'So, VINTAGE ROSES, express delivery?'

'Yes. They need to go straight away.'

The pretty assistant—Marie, according to the badge pinned to the front of her apron—was pouting a little. *Flirting!* Usually, he'd have flirted back but instead he was drifting, sliding into the dark green depths of Simone Cossart's eyes. He couldn't see past her sweet face, that lush, kissable mouth—

'Did you have a colour in mind, *monsieur*?'

He blinked. 'What have you got?'

'Pink, mauve, cream, and apricot.'

Which colour would Simone like? Her coat had been black, her dress grey. That wasn't much to go on. What had Amy said about her apartment, that she'd made the best of it but that it was dreary and chilly and dated? Amy hadn't mentioned a colour, just a dripping tap! He felt his neck prickling. Landlords shouldn't have been allowed to let out places like that. They should have been forced to maintain things! In his line, things *had* to work. It was a life-or-death thing—

'*Monsieur?*'

Marie's face came back, instantly morphing into Simone's...that blush in her cheeks, the disbelief in her eyes when he'd offered her his hat. Such a small thing, and yet she'd looked as if he'd been giving her the world, a world she thought she didn't deserve. It was only a hat, one of many that his sponsors sent by the boxful on a regular basis. He took a breath. 'Let's go for ten of each and please send them as an arrangement in a cylinder vase.' Slicing and crushing the stem tips of forty roses would have turned his gift into a chore, and gifts weren't meant to be hard work. 'Plain crystal, I think.'

'Certainly, *monsieur.*'

'And I'll need a card.'

Marie pulled out a box of cards from under the long green counter. He thumbed through, picking a cream card with a simple tooled border. Nothing fussy. Simone wasn't the fussy type. She'd looked elegant in her plain grey dress and long black boots. No frills, no adornments, but she'd stolen his breath away all the same. He was still trying to get it back.

Marie tucked the box away. 'We can print the card for you—'

'No, thanks. I'm going for the personal touch.' He pulled out his pen, flashing his eyebrows. 'Means more, right?'

She nodded, returning a wistful smile.

He moved to the end of the counter and clicked the pen. What to write? How to translate his chaotic feelings into words?

He'd gone to the bistro with one thing in mind: to persuade Simone to be Yannick's childminder for Christmas. What he hadn't expected was to feel attracted to her, and he definitely hadn't expected to feel so moved by her gentle empathy. He'd thought that opening up was going to be one-way traffic, him pouring everything out, making his case, but what he'd seen in her eyes while he'd been talking, what he'd felt flowing back had drawn him in somehow and now he was in a tangle. Being drawn in— *where?*—was absolutely not his comfort zone. He didn't do intimacy, didn't want to dangle himself on the end of anyone's strings, or dangle anyone on the end of his. He'd felt enough pain in his life to know that he never wanted to inflict it on anyone else. It was why he always kept his encounters with women honest—purely physical—only ever going with women of the same mindset, like Zara. No strings, no ties. *Ironic!*

And yet, talking to Simone had felt like being in a kind of comfort zone. She'd made things easy, made him feel safe and he was so, so grateful. It was why he was here, why he'd sprinted all the way from the bistro to catch the florists before they closed. He wanted her to feel his gratitude, wanted to give her something that would light up her lovely face, and cheer up her dreary apartment. Tenderness bloomed in his chest. He'd always felt guilty about being rich and privileged, even though he'd exploited it, but now he was glad that he could afford to send Simone forty vintage roses in a crystal vase, express delivery.

He ran his eyes over the buckets of colourful blooms. His mother, Colette, had always filled their apartment with exotic lilies and richly scented roses. Always the best, the most expensive. Maybe he'd inherited the gene! Hopefully, it was the only one, or was that unfair? A sharp ache lanced him between the temples. Who knew? Colette had always confused him. *Hurt him!* Capricious. Generous. Selfish. Which label fitted her best? All of them or none? He swallowed hard feeling a familiar stab of resentment. He hadn't bothered asking her to help him out over Christmas. She wouldn't even have considered it. For some inexplicable reason, Colette hated Chamonix, and her sentiments had always overruled his needs. He clenched his teeth. Why was he even thinking about her? She didn't merit the energy, whereas Simone…

He closed his eyes, felt his pulse climbing. Kissing her goodbye, feeling her skin against his lips had almost undone him because he'd wanted to pull her close and kiss her mouth instead. He'd wanted to take down her hair, wreak some havoc—

'Monsieur!' Marie's gaze was firm. 'I'm sorry but if you want delivery today, then I'm going to need the card.'

'Of course. I'm sorry.'

He squared up the card. Whatever Simone was doing to him, for Yann's sake, and for the sake of his career, he had to stow it. He needed her to say yes to Chamonix, and that meant staying focused, using everything in his power to persuade her. She was a good parent, dashing off so she wouldn't be late for Chloe, putting Chloe first. He clicked the pen. He didn't know how that felt, to be put first, but it was what he was trying to do with Yann…

He felt an ache in his throat. He didn't love Yann, but he wanted to, wanted to give him love, and attention, and time, all the things he'd never had. And he wanted to feel love flowing back, see Yann's eyes lighting up when he came in. He wanted to feel Yann diving into his arms as kids did with their *papa* in movies. He wanted to be a good father, and Simone could help him. She *had* to come to Chamonix.

He anchored the card with his fingers, drew in a long breath and wrote.

Thank you! Dax.

Simone gazed at the roses, flexing the card in her fingers. Pastel perfection! The most gorgeous flowers she'd ever received from anyone, including André. And already in a vase so there was nothing for her to do but look at them! She felt her eyes welling, a smile wobbling onto her lips. *Dax!* First his hat, and now this...

She looked at the card again. Handwritten. Big generous loops. Not the florist's writing. His, surely. He must have gone to the florist himself, straight after, picked out the colours, the card, everything. Thank you for what, though? For meeting him? For considering his proposal?

She propped the card against the vase then buried her hands into the sleeves of her cardigan. The proposal was simple enough. It was everything else that wasn't. It had been hard watching Dax wading through all that personal stuff just to explain why he needed her and Chloe to go to Chamonix. His eyes had been full of hurt and frustration, desperation, determination and then, as they'd said goodbye, hope.

She sighed. She'd carried his hope all the way back to the Metro, had felt its weight pressing down on her as she'd watched Chloe pointing her pink satin toes through the final moments of her ballet class. It was here now, mingling with the fragrance of his roses, shimmering through the air around her, but she couldn't let it cloud her judgement. Yes, for Chloe, a snowy Christmas in the mountains with her best friend would be a huge treat, and yes, the money would be great. The problem was that even though Dax seemed nice— more than nice—she didn't *know* him, and, even taking into account the extenuating circumstances, going away for Christmas with a man she'd only met once seemed rash.

She bit her lips together. Except she wouldn't be *going away with a man*. That was the wrong emphasis, her own feelings tangling things up because of what had happened between them at the bistro door, the thing that they'd somehow glossed over and tucked away. She sighed. It was what she needed to do now, tuck away the flutters and the tingles and weigh things up objectively. Dax was offering to pay her whatever she wanted for taking care of his sad little boy in Chamonix, and Chloe would love to go, definitely! The alternative was faking Christmas cheer at the farm, pretending to Maman that life in Paris wasn't paper-thin.

She felt a cold lump shifting in the pit of her stomach. If Maman and Papa hadn't been tied to the farm, they'd have come to visit, seen the apartment, seen how unhappy she was. *There!* She'd admitted it, and if she could admit that Paris wasn't the same without André, that her dreams had died with him on that crossing, then, where did that leave her? Where did she want to be? Definitely not in Charente, married to a farmer, which was what Maman wanted for her. Avoiding that fate was one of the reasons why she'd come to Paris in the first place!

She pulled her hands out of her sleeves and rubbed her temples. Could she find the magic in it again? She wanted to, desperately, because Paris was André's city. She wanted Chloe to experience it, to live it and breathe it as he had. André *was* Paris. All her memories of him were here, memories she wanted Chloe to feel. Happy memories! Life *had* been good before. Yes, falling pregnant with Chloe had scuppered her own musical ambitions, and yes, they hadn't exactly planned on getting married at twenty-two, but they'd been in love, and so incredibly happy. Her in-laws had helped them out with the rent on a decent apartment and, just months before he died, André had been accepted into the Paris Orchestra. They'd been on their way…

She swallowed hard, tuning in to the drip of the tap. *Bloody thing!* But this apartment wasn't for ever! Things *were* getting better. The school job meant regular money and a place for Chloe, a place she'd never have been able to afford otherwise! A better apartment was on the cards too. She was turning a corner. Selling her violin to help make ends meet had felt like a body blow, but soon she'd be able to buy a replacement and get back to giving lessons. Having a proper job was only the start! It was opening doors. It had already opened Dax's…

'I haven't been pulling my weight for my sponsors. I need to get back to it, honour my commitments.'

Free riding was as important to Dax as playing the violin had been to her, even if she couldn't quite visualise what 'lines' were or why sponsors paid him to ride them.

'…if you want to see what I do, you could watch one of my films.'

Of course! How could she have forgotten? She felt a tingle travelling along her spine. When Chloe was in bed, she'd fire up

André's old laptop and find out exactly why Dax D'Aureval was a movie star!

She typed Dax's name into the search bar. Instantly the screen filled. Articles. Photos. Dax, tanned and smiling, making her pulse flutter. She went to a profile piece, speed reading. He had a lot of sponsors. Snowboard manufacturers; winter sports clothing brands; a Swiss watch maker…tracking devices… GPS phones…a climbing equipment crowd. *Why?* Surely snowboarding was about coming down, not climbing up!

She shrugged inside her head, clicking links. *What?* Was that him spooning dollops of yoghurt into a bowl? She cranked the volume, feeling a giggle starting. He was smiling into the camera, completely gorgeous in a plain white tee. *'If you're as active as I am, you need to pack in the protein…'* She giggled, watching as the picture cut to him somersaulting on his board. He *was* good! No wonder he was getting advertising deals. *Films!*

She settled the computer on her knees, clicking through to a video site. *Wow!* They really *did* make films about him, lots of films! *Ice Rider*; *Taming Alaska with Dax D'Aureval*; *Free-Riding Hacks with Dax*; *Whispering Slopes* and *Frozen Line*. That would do!

She clicked play. A tense, tingling refrain started as blackness faded up into a breathtaking aerial shot of snowy slopes and jagged peaks, edged pink by the rising sun that beamed its rays out of the screen as the camera panned round. *Chamonix!* When the camera—it could only have been a drone—breached an edge and dropped, her stomach dropped with it, and then she was travelling along the splintered side of an icy cliff. The music dipped, and suddenly Dax was speaking, his voice low and calm.

'I've studied Mallory Couloir many times, looking for a way to make it mine, to find a line that no one else has found. And now, I have...'

She felt her mouth falling open as the camera closed in on a figure—*Dax*—sliding his board sideways down a face that looked near vertical. He was wearing a helmet, and he was roped, anchored to a place higher up, letting out the rope as he went, his board scraping ice.

Suddenly his face filled the screen, eyebrows flashing, a smile twitching on his lips. *'Intense, huh?'*

The picture zoomed out, and her breath caught. He *was* on a vertical face, him and the crew that were filming him. Were they all mad?

His face filled the frame again. He was blowing out quick breaths, grimacing a bit, talking to the camera but maybe also to himself.

'Whew, whew! Breathe!'

And then the camera tailed him as he slid his board along a narrow ice shelf, digging a pair of sharp axes into the face above as he went. *Axes!* What if he fell on his axe? She curled her fingers into her palms.

The shimmering music shifted into a lower key as the view changed. He was riding now, weaving tightly over powder snow, axes in his hands, but the slope was still sickeningly vertical. When the view switched back to aerial, she bit her knuckles. He was like an ant against the white colossus of the mountain. Small. *Vulnerable.* And then he was wearing ropes again, lowering himself down another impossible face. Suddenly the mountaineering equipment sponsorship made sense!

And then he was on snow, a bullet in a red jacket hurtling down a vertical gully, free falling metres at a time before catching the slope again. The music faded and there was his voice again, slightly defiant.

'When I'm riding, there's a spirit inside me that is wild, definitely a little crazy...'

A *little* crazy? He was certifiable! But she couldn't look away, even though her heart was racing, and her mouth was dry. Dax's power and agility were mesmerising. He looked sexy as hell. She *had* to keep watching.

The music was growing jauntier, matching the rhythm of his quick weaving movements. He was throwing up flurries, launching himself off spurs, sailing through the air with joyful hyena cries, and then he was hammering down the mountain, the view switching to his helmet camera and she was right there with him, feeling the rush of the slope, hearing the scrunch and swish of the board, feeling white blinded, blue dazzled, snow and sky flying towards her at breakneck speed.

And then the picture changed to a wide view from a lower angle. Dax was racing down the corrugated mountain, racing mini avalanches that were exploding into life on either side of him. He stayed ahead, slicing across the snowfield, somersaulting—sky rotating into snow, snow rotating into sky—whooping and hollering, and then he was coming in fast, slewing to a halt inches from the camera. He ripped off his goggles, eyes bright as fever. 'Now, *that's* what I'm talking about!'

She slumped back, blowing out a long breath. So *that* was free riding? It was amazing, and terrifying, and— The air in her lungs solidified. *This* was what he was going to be doing in Chamonix? *This* was why he needed her to be there? She felt a band tightening around her chest, a fluttering panic. He'd said something about an expedition. Was it going to be like the one she'd just watched...ropes, axes, vertical cliffs? She looked at the screen. Another film was playing, more of the same. She hit the cross. He couldn't do this, couldn't *keep on* doing this! It was too dangerous. One slip, one wrong move...

She shoved the computer off her lap and rocked forwards, pressing her fingertips into her forehead. What was he thinking? He was a father! That meant changing, making sacrifices. Carrying on was selfish. Completely irresponsible! For pity's sake, Yann had already lost his mother!

She squeezed her eyes shut, anger rising. He'd been kitted out and roped up. He'd seemed confident, but accidents happened. By definition they were unexpected. He could lose his balance, fall into a crevasse, slide off an edge. A rope could snap, a karabiner could sheer... Those mini avalanches could have turned themselves into giants. Dax could be buried alive. He could die, and then what? What would happen to Yannick?

Suddenly she couldn't breathe. Her throat was burning, clogging with bitterness, the old pain searing her insides all over again. She got to her feet, gulping breaths, tears scalding her eyes. André had been killed three Christmases ago by a driver who'd been texting instead of watching the road. His life had been snuffed out, and a good part of hers with it, and there was Dax, a father as well, asking her to look after Yannick while he spent Christmas risking his life for the sake of what, an adrenaline rush?

No! A sob felled her. *No way!* It was wrong. *Wrong!* She wouldn't do it; wouldn't facilitate it.

She swallowed hard, sitting back on her heels, shuddering breaths, smearing the tears into her cheeks. All that hope in his eyes…and the hat… and the flowers… But she couldn't sanction the thing he loved, and she'd have to tell him, just as soon as she was calm enough to make the call.

Dax tapped the arrow key, rotating the satellite image on his screen by degrees. Aiguille du Plan looked scary from the top, and scary from below, but its ambivalence was magnetic. He wanted to conquer it, look out from its splintered sides, see views that few had the privilege to see. He felt a sudden tearing ache in his chest. He missed the mountains. In the mountains his senses had meaning, his mind was free. Here everything was chaos. He had no control. He couldn't make Yann like him, couldn't make him happy. Why couldn't he find the right line with Yann?

His phone jumped, vibrating on the desk. An unfamiliar number. He swiped right. 'Hello?'

'Dax?'

'Simone!' Warmth streamed through his veins, apprehension galloping behind. Had she made a decision about Chamonix? He leant back in his chair, trying to sound mellow. 'How are you? Did you make it to Chloe in time?'

'I'm fine thanks and yes, I made it.' Her voice filled with a smile. 'Thank you for the roses, Dax. They're so, so beautiful.'

'You're welcome. I'm glad you like them.' He couldn't help smiling. Dashing to the florist's had been a happy distraction from worrying about Yannick, and his career, and his sponsors. All the obligations he was going to have to juggle from now on.

'So, Dax…'

His heart pulsed. Her voice was downshifting. He swallowed, trying to keep his tone even. 'Yes?'

'I…erm…'

He squeezed his eyes shut, bracing himself.

'I've been thinking about Chamonix, and, on reflection, I've decided that, much as I'd like to say yes, I can't disappoint my parents.'

Parents?

'Chloe and I always go there for Christmas. They farm in Charente. It's very tying so they never get to visit us in Paris, which means they don't see much of Chloe. Us going there is important.'

No! Her parents had each other. They didn't need her, not as *he* needed her, not as Yannick needed her.

Her voice was catching a little. 'I came to meet you because I promised Amy I would. I wanted to give you my consideration…but I just feel that I can't let my parents down. I'm sorry.'

He felt his heart shrivelling. What was he going to do now? Some of his Chamonix friends had kids. Maybe he could ask… *No!* They were *his* friends, not Yannick's. To Yann they'd be strangers and no way was he leaving Yann with strangers! Not leaving his son with strangers was exactly why he'd laid out his whole sorry history for Simone, so she'd see that she and Chloe were the only ones who could help him. But now…? He stared at the rocky pinnacle on his computer screen. He was going to have to shelve Aiguille du Plan, let everyone down, as he'd let them down over his Alaskan adventure. His stomach cramped. Letting people down wasn't him! It was Colette's way, not *his*.

'Dax?'

He blinked.

'Are you still there?' There was an anxious pause. 'I feel bad. I *am* really, really sorry…'

She really *did* feel bad. He could hear it. He felt his pulse gathering. Maybe this wasn't over. It wasn't as if she'd called him as soon as she'd got home. He flicked a glance at his watch. Nine-thirty! She'd been thinking about it for almost five hours. And she *had* come to meet him, hadn't she? She'd known what he was proposing because Amy had already told her. She hadn't been thinking about her parents *then*. What had she said as she'd been leaving? *'I'm leaning towards yes...'* How close had she been at that moment? He ran his tongue over his lower lip. Was there still a chance he could change her mind? There were still a few days to play with. There was nothing to lose...

He inhaled slowly, sliding behind cut-out Dax. 'Please, Simone, don't feel bad. It's my problem, not yours.' He squeezed his eyes shut, hating himself for being disingenuous. 'I'm only sorry that you and Chloe won't be with us in the mountains. It's truly magical at Christmas.'

CHAPTER THREE

December 8th...

'RUE VICTOR-HUGO, PLEASE.' Simone sat back, drawing in a slow breath. Her heart was drumming and, in spite of her big coat and the muggy warmth inside the taxi, small shivers were running up and down her spine.

Stupid nerves!

She glanced at the meter then looked through the window. A taxi was the only way to get to Dax's apartment and back in her lunch break so torturing herself about the cost was pointless. She scanned the boulevard, trying to distract herself, but it was no good. She couldn't stop turning it over. Dax had finally done it, pushed her into a corner, and now she had to push back, spell it out face to face once and for all: she was not going to Chamonix for Christmas, no matter how many flowers and gifts he sent. The plumber who'd arrived at stupid o'clock that morning to fix her tap had been the last straw. If Dax wasn't listening, she'd have to make him.

She chewed her lips, watching the pale elegant buildings slip by. How had she got herself into this impossible situation? She sighed. By being too soft, that was how! If she'd been honest from the start, told Dax exactly what she thought of his risk-taking, instead of trying to soften the blow with the whole *We always go to my parents for Christmas* routine, adding extra layers of, *I feel bad... I'm so sorry*, then none of this would have been happening.

She sighed again. It was just that by the time she'd calmed down, it had felt too harsh to be calling Dax out on his lifestyle choices. After all, she barely knew him, and he *was* the father of Chloe's best friend. It had seemed best to give him a credible excuse that wouldn't sour things for them, or the kids. *Mistake!* All she'd done was leave him a gap to squeeze through!

The next day a lavish arrangement of sugar-pink roses and stargazer lilies had arrived. This time he'd written, by hand:

Thank you for thinking about it at least.
Dax

She twisted the strap of her bag around her fingers, watching the windows of the fancy Champs-élysées boutiques spinning by. *Dax!* So gorgeous. So generous. So transparent! He hadn't been thanking her; he'd been forcing her to engage.

'Hi, Dax.'

'*Simone!*' *Brimming warmth.* '*How are you today?*'

'*I'm fine. I'm just calling to say thank you—again—for the beautiful flowers.*'

'*My pleasure.*'

'*You really shouldn't have sent them—*'

'*But I wanted to thank you.*'

Small hesitation.

'*You said you felt bad about Chamonix and I can't have that. The Chamonix situation is for me to deal with, not for you to feel bad about.*'

Small hesitation, confessional tone.

'*To be honest, I feel bad for asking you in the first place. I was desperate, but it was unfair of me to put you in that position. I hope you can forgive me?*'

'*It's fine, Dax, honestly.*'

Long sigh.

'*I'm relieved...because Yann really does love Chloe. I wouldn't want my mistake to change anything. She's all he has.*'

'*Nothing's going to change, okay, but please, don't send any more flowers.*'

Lighter tone.

'*Okay. I promise. No more flowers.*'

She freed her fingers and opened her bag, taking out her lipstick. *Warpaint!* She applied it carefully, checking her teeth, then slipped it back.

If Dax had stopped then, things would have settled, but he hadn't. The next day a pink goose-down ski jacket had arrived…for Chloe! One of Dax's sponsor's brands, top of the range.

His handwritten note had said:

Hope you don't mind me sending this. It was supposed to be blue, for Yannick, but they sent the wrong colour. I thought Chloe might like it.
Dax

She'd felt blindsided. Chloe had pounced on the jacket, parading around in it like a mini cat-walk model, flicking up the fur-trimmed hood then flicking it back with a giggling head toss. Simone had had to laugh, even though she was furious. Sending Chloe a gift was a calculated move, and, of course, it had meant calling him again. She'd made Chloe say thank you first, then she'd taken over.

'Dax, it's a really beautiful jacket so thank you. Chloe's thrilled, but if you think that it's going to change anything, then I'm afraid you're wrong.'

'I'm sorry?'

Confused tone.

'It's a winter jacket. For winter sports. It's the kind of jacket a little girl would wear if she were going to, let's say...hmm... Chamonix?'

'Simone!'

Incredulous tone laced with amusement.

'Are you accusing me of bribery?' Heavy sigh. *'Look, it's a winter jacket because my sponsors make winter jackets!'*

Low, mischievous tone.

'If I'd been trying to bribe you, I would have been far more imaginative.'

Her neck prickled at the memory. Had the jacket really been an innocent gift? Even now she didn't know. She'd apologised for the mis-understanding and ended the call in a haze of confusion.

She closed her eyes. *Dax!* Confusing her at every turn. She didn't approve of him, but there was something undeniably warm about him, something about him that was pulling her this way and that, night, and day. She couldn't stop remembering the way he'd looked at her at the bistro door, the sensuality that shimmered around him like phosphorescence. In his eyes, in his smile, in the way he held himself, even in the way he sipped espresso. She couldn't stop imagining how his lips would feel on hers, warm and perfect, how his skin would feel next to hers if they were naked, wrapped together warm and close and—

The taxi lurched. She came to, cheeks burning. What was wrong with her? André was the one she ought to have been fantasising about, André, who'd snatched her heart away under the enigmatic gaze of the Mona Lisa. Dax didn't come close! Dax was a practised charmer, a player, a selfish adrenaline junkie, and she needed to remember that! It was why he'd sent the plumber, but it was one plumber too many. She'd had enough of being toyed with. Telling him why she'd really turned down his proposal was the last thing she wanted to do, but if it came to it, she would, if he gave her no choice…

'Hey, Dax!' Amy's voice broke his concentration. 'Simone's here!'

Simone?

He twisted his head, felt his breath catching on a smile. She was standing next to Amy, looking up at him with red, slightly parted lips. He gripped the handholds hard, felt his heart pumping. Was she here to say that she was coming to Cham after all? Did he even dare to hope? He climbed down a notch, then jumped clear of the wall, dusting the chalk off his hands as he walked over.

'Hello!' He kissed her cheeks. 'This is a nice surprise.'

'Hi!' Her eyes locked on his. 'I'm sorry if I'm disturbing you.'

'You're not.' Not in the way she meant, anyway. Her steady gaze was wrecking his pulse and as for her ruby mouth... He swallowed, motioning to the wall. 'As you can see, I was just hanging around...'

'Without ropes!'

She looked so serious that he couldn't resist a little mischief. He flashed his eyebrows. 'I like to live dangerously.'

A smile ghosted on her lips and then it faded. His heart caved. If he couldn't stir a smile out of her, then she definitely wasn't here to accept his offer.

'Would you like some tea, Simone?' Amy was hooking his tee shirt off the bench press, handing it to him with a pointed *Cover yourself* look, and then she turned back to Simone. 'Or some coffee?'

'No, thanks. You're busy, and besides, I'm not staying.' Her eyes came back to his. 'I just need to speak to Dax for a moment.'

A moment? He toyed with his tee shirt. If that was all she should have phoned instead of getting his hopes up. It wasn't as if she hadn't called him twice already, about the flowers and about Chloe's jacket! *Oh, God!* Was this about the plumber? Had he gone too far? He hadn't meant to. It was just Amy had said the dripping tap got on Simone's nerves, and since things that didn't work got on his nerves too, he'd sent someone—

'Okay then...' Amy was backstepping. 'I need to get on with my packing.'

He gave her a nod, felt a knot tightening inside. She was leaving in the morning, leaving him at the helm, and he still didn't know what to do about Christmas. He'd held off booking flights, hoping that he'd be booking four seats not two, but something was telling him he was out of luck. He sighed and pulled on his tee shirt. 'Are you sure I can't get you anything, Simone, a soft drink maybe?'

'I'm fine, but thanks.' She took a step, looking past him. 'You've got your own climbing wall.'

'Hasn't everyone?'

Her eyebrows flickered but she didn't smile.

His chest went tight. What was wrong with her? Or...was it him? Flashing his eyebrows, making quips that effectively cut conversation dead? Classic cut-out Dax! He rubbed his arm, cleaning off a streak of chalk. The last time he'd been with her, he'd been himself, and she'd been warm and full of kindness. If he wanted that Simone back, if he wanted to know what was on her mind, then he had to drop the act.

He took a breath and went to the wall, curling his fingers around one of the holds. 'I put in my own wall because I can change the holds around whenever I want. I like to keep challenging myself.' He turned, meeting her gaze. 'I'm energetic by nature. Some would say hyperactive!' He shrugged. 'Bottom line, if there wasn't a climbing wall in here, I'd be climbing the walls anyway.'

The light in her eyes softened a little. 'You're very agile. I saw that in your film.'

'You watched one of my films?' For some reason he felt stoked. 'Which one?'

'Frozen Line.'

'Ah, Mallory Couloir! We made that last year!' When his life had been *his*. He pushed the thought away. 'Riding that line was crazy scary.'

'Is that why you do it?' Her gaze sharpened. 'For thrills?'

He felt a stab of resentment. Was she judging him? He didn't deserve that. He measured out a breath, keeping his voice level. 'Tell me, Simone, do you have a favourite food?'

Her eyebrows arched. 'Hasn't everyone?'

In spite of himself, he felt his lips twitching. '*Touché*, Madame Cossart!' And then suddenly there seemed to be a spark in her eyes too. This was better. Much better. He shifted on his feet. 'So what is it? What's your favourite?'

She gave a little shrug. 'I don't see the relevance.'

'You will.' He held in a smile. 'Please, just answer the question.'

She pouted a little. 'I like flan.'

'What do you like about it? Break it down.'

Her eyes widened. 'Really?'

Fighting all the way! He dipped his chin. 'Yes.'

She let out a sigh. 'I suppose it's the taste—vanilla—the sweetness, the smooth texture, the way the pastry crumbles. All of it!'

'Everything, then?'

She nodded.

'So it's the same for me with free riding.' He took a step towards her. 'It's thrilling, absolutely, but I don't only do it for thrills. It's bigger. It's the challenge. It's simply being in the mountains. It's the snow. It's the ice. It's that special silence, and the big sky. Up there, you feel the very tips of your senses.' He felt a smile loosening his cheeks. 'Free riding feels like nothing else on earth. I love it, and I'm good at it, and I'll always want to do it, like you'll always want to eat flan.'

Her eyes were glimmering. What was she thinking? Suddenly he couldn't stand it. 'Simone, why are you here?'

She blinked. 'To thank you for sending the

plumber, and for your kindness.' Her gaze tightened on his. 'But I also want to know what you're expecting to come of it, because it seems to me that maybe you're expecting something…?'

His chest went tight. 'No, no, I'm not.' He felt a drag of weariness. 'I was just hoping, that's all, hoping to sway you…' Hoping to save Yann from having to suffer his presence over Christmas without a buffer, without a friend there to make him happy. Hoping to save his career, because leaving Yann with some random childminder while he went on the slopes was out of the question.

'There's nothing you can do to sway me, Dax.' She was shaking her head slowly, her eyes softer now. 'So please, stop trying.'

No! He felt desperation boiling up inside, taking him over. 'Please, Simone, please reconsider. I need to be on the slopes, not for the thrill of it, but because I've got obligations, commitments. It's how I make my living.' The only one that mattered anyway.

She was opening her mouth to speak, but he couldn't let her interrupt. Selling it hard was the only way, because if she didn't help him, he'd have to call everything off so he could be there for Yann twenty-four-seven. He'd do it, of course he would, but Yann would be miserable, and his own reputation would be ruined.

He took a step towards her. 'Look, what I'm asking you to do won't feel like work. It'll feel like a holiday!' A tiny spark lit her gaze. She was listening. He felt his love for his home rising like a tide. 'My chalet is on its own high up in the mountains. The views are awesome. And it's luxurious. All mod cons! There's a pool, and a hot tub. Oh, and in case you're wondering, I have a housekeeper who comes in to cook and clean, so no chores! And I can set up cool activities for the kids, like ski school...' Something flickered behind her eyes. Of course, Chloe was her Achilles heel, as Yann was his. He licked his lips. 'Has Chloe ever skied?'

She shook her head.

'So wouldn't this be the perfect opportunity for her to try!' Now she was really paying attention. He swallowed. 'And if she doesn't like skiing there's always tobogganing or ice skating. And there are things we could all do together if you wanted to.'

Would she want that? He just needed to keep talking.

'Dog sledding is fun! The kids would love it, and there's a Christmas market, and cool shops! Cham is magical at Christmas.' He took another step towards her, loading his gaze. 'Wouldn't

you like to give Chloe a magical Christmas?'
Her eyes were clouding, growing hazy. He
looked at her mouth, felt his pulse quickening.
'I'll pay you whatever you want plus expenses,
whatever it has to be to make it work. Just say
you'll come. Please.'

For a long second her eyes held his and then
she was stepping back, shaking her head. 'No.'

'Why?' It came out hoarsely. He swallowed
hard. 'Because of your parents? Forgive me, but
I'm struggling to believe that's the reason.' She
was blinking, her throat working. 'For pity's
sake, Simone, why won't you help me?'

She looked away for a beat, and then her eyes
snapped back to his. 'Because when you kill
yourself, Dax, I don't want to be the one who
has to tell Yannick that his *papa* thought riding
a snowboard down a cliff was more important
than being a father!'

Her words hit him like a slap. For a moment
he was breathless, disorientated. He'd never
even thought of that! The mountains were dangerous. It was why he took every precaution but
dying wasn't on his radar. It was a distant pos-
sibility. Unreal. As it was for anyone. He felt
an ache bouncing between his temples. What
would Simone have him do? Give up everything he was, everything he'd ever loved for a
son he'd never asked for, a son who didn't even

like him and probably never would? And would giving up even make Yann happy? It was too big to think about under the burn of her gaze.

'I'm sorry.' He stepped back, tasting the dryness in his mouth. 'I won't ask again.' He turned and went over to the water cooler, feeling despair aching through his veins. Was it so wrong, to want to carry on doing the thing he loved? Couldn't he be a free rider and a father? He tugged two paper cups from the dispenser, filling them in turn. Simone didn't think so, and for some annoying reason what she thought mattered. He sighed. Simone was a proper grown-up. She was strong and sensible and kind. And he was, what? He threw back a cupful of water. Without his snowboard, he was nothing.

He drew in a deep breath then went back over, offering her a cup. 'How about some water?'

'Thanks.' She took it, sipping slowly, and then she looked up, her gaze softer now. 'I didn't want to say it, you know, but you weren't giving up, so I had to.' She sighed. 'How you live is obviously up to you, Dax, but I can't not feel what I feel…' She drained her cup then handed it to him. 'I've got to go. I'm on my lunch break.'

'How are you getting back?'

'Taxi.'

'No, you're not!' The least he could do was take her back. Whatever she thought of him, she was still the mother of Yann's best friend, and he liked her, didn't want there to be any awkwardness between them. 'I'll run you back.'

She tilted her head, eyes narrowing. 'You're not still trying—'

'No!' No matter how devastated he was feeling about Christmas, he absolutely wasn't going to bring it up with her again. He smiled. 'I promise.'

'This is yours?' Simone was staring at the SUV with raised eyebrows.

Maybe she'd been expecting a sports car, something fast. Five months ago she'd have been right. He opened the passenger door, stepping back. 'I had something sexier before, but it wasn't family friendly, so it had to go.' He flicked a glance at the wing. 'I think it might have been better in red, but Yann likes blue.'

She was looking at him as if he'd said something profound, and then she smiled quickly and got in. 'The blue's nice.'

'It's okay.' He closed her door, tailing round to the driver's side. If Yann had ever enthused about the colour it would have felt like a win, but he hadn't. Yann seemed to be as ambivalent about the car as he was.

He got in, reaching for his seat belt.

'Wait!'

He turned, felt his breath catching. Simone was looking at him softly, her eyes full of warm light. He felt it reaching in, turning him inside out. He swallowed. 'What's up?'

She pressed her lips together. 'I just wanted to say that, for what it's worth, I thought your film was amazing.'

Amazing!

'You blew me away, Dax. I don't like what you do, the risks you take, in fact, I think you're insane, but you're really good at it.' Her cheeks were colouring. 'I admire you.'

Her honesty was astounding. Humbling. He drew in a careful breath. Was there any mileage to be made—? *No!* He'd promised he wouldn't try persuading her again, and whatever his other failings were, breaking promises wasn't one of them.

He pushed the seat belt home and started the engine. 'Thank you.' He felt a smile edging onto his lips. 'It means a lot that you think I'm insane!' He pulled out, catching her smile in the wing mirror. Smiling suited her. Smiling made her eyes shine, yet most of the time she seemed serious, and a little sad. She was a widow, but Amy didn't know how she'd lost her husband. He was curious but asking didn't feel right. It wasn't as if they were proper friends, people who'd come together naturally—

'The taxi didn't go this way!'

'Really?' The note of indignation in her voice was too tempting. He looked over, felt his lips twitching. 'Maybe the taxi took you the scenic route.'

Her eyes flew wide. 'You think?'

He chuckled. 'No! I'm teasing. This is just the way I go. I grew up in Paris, so I know a few short cuts.' He looked ahead. Ribbons of snow still edged the bare branches of the trees lining the boulevard, but the gutters were thick with dirty slush. Parisian snow! So different from alpine snow. He felt a pang, a sudden need to keep talking. 'I haven't lived here for years. I don't like it really.' A memory flashed: Colette's soirées. He shuddered. 'I left when I was sixteen, took off travelling. In Alaska I hopped on a snowboard and that was it! I was smitten. After that, I was always on the move, chasing snow, then I built my place in Cham, travelled out from there...' He bit his lips together. 'Of course, that's all changed. Now I'm back.'

'Why?' She was twisting in her seat, angling herself towards him. 'Why did you come back if you don't like it?'

'Because I was in a flat spin, thinking about good schools, thinking that my mother would—' A knot yanked tight in his belly. Did he really want to be getting into this? *Yes!* Simone was a gentle ear and for once in his life he wanted to let it all out. He looked over. 'Because it's instinctive, isn't it, running home when you're in trouble, when you need someone to lean on?' He fixed his eyes on the road again, feeling the old bruise starting to swell. 'True to form, my mother hasn't exactly fallen over herself, unless you count giving me the apartment, which was, of course, *very* generous. Gifts always were Colette's forte! She wasn't so good at—' He bit his tongue. *Enough!* If he carried on bleating, maybe she'd think he was courting sympathy, trying to persuade her to help him yet again and he wasn't.

'At what?'

He looked over. Simone's gaze was soft, full of ready empathy. He gave a little shrug, going for a nonchalant tone. 'She just wasn't very hands-on.'

'What about your father? Was he—?'

'He wasn't around.' He looked ahead, felt the knot in his stomach twisting. 'I don't even know who he is.' He felt her silent question humming through air. 'Yes, I asked my mother, and no, she doesn't know.'

'I'm so sorry.'

He felt her hand on his shoulder fleetingly, her eyes combing his face. If she was looking for tears, she was wasting her time. It didn't hurt. He wasn't curious. He had been once, but that was a long time ago. 'Thanks, but it's okay. It is what it is. Ironic!'

'What? That you don't know your father and nearly didn't know your son?'

'Yep!' He met her eye. 'At least Yann knows who I am and who he looks like. He knows I'm here for him.' He forced a smile out. 'I just need to crack the whole parenting thing and then we'll be fine.' He turned the SUV into the school road and pulled in by the gates. 'Here you go, back to school safe and sound.'

'Thank you.' She put her hand on the door, and then she turned, her eyes full of light and kindness. 'You'll get there with Yann, Dax, it's just going to take time, that's all.'

Time and a whole bunch of miracles! But it was his problem now, and his alone. He cracked his door open. 'Sit tight. I'll get your door.'

'There's no need.'

'Yes, there is.' Anything to delay saying good-bye, to delay being alone with his turmoil, to delay being without her. He held her gaze for as long as he dared and then he smiled. 'I might be insane, but I like to think I'm a gentleman too.'

CHAPTER FOUR

Later...

'MAMAN, DO YOU like snow? Because I *love* snow.'

Dax shimmered into her head. That moment at the bistro door, pulling off his hat, showering snow...that moment in his gym, half naked, dusting off his hands, showering chalk—

'Maman?'

She blinked, steadying the laptop on her knees. 'You know I do.'

'Snow makes everything Christmassy!' Chloe was drawing, leaning over the coffee table in a scatter of crayons. 'I *love* Christmas. You love it too, don't you?'

She slipped a smile into her voice. 'Of course I do. Everyone loves Christmas.'

Lying to Chloe about Christmas was second nature. Chloe didn't know the date of André's death, or the details, and she wasn't in a rush to tell her. She watched her daughter's fair hair swinging, her busy little hands moving over the paper. Maybe she never would.

Chloe looked up suddenly. 'Can we put the Christmas tree up tomorrow?'

'Absolutely!' The artificial tree she'd had to settle for because dragging a real one up seven flights wasn't an option! Maybe the access in their new place would be easier, then they could go back to having a real tree with all the nice piney smells. She smiled. 'We'll put it up as soon as we get back from school. It can be our way of celebrating the end of term!'

Chloe's eyes lit with a smile. 'I love you, Maman.'

'I love you too, *chérie*.' So much!

Chloe went back to drawing and she turned back to the picture on her screen: a team of frisky huskies pulling a laughing couple along in a sled through sparkling snow. Her heart twisted. Chloe loved dogs, would love riding behind huskies...

Impossible!

She shut the laptop. She'd given Dax her decision, and it was the right decision—wasn't it?—even if it meant that Chloe wouldn't get to go dog sledding or stay in a mountain chalet with all the mod cons!

She pushed the laptop aside and got up. 'Would you like some hot chocolate?'

'Ooh, yes, please!' Chloe was colouring in fiercely.

'Okay…one hot chocolate coming up!'

She went into the kitchen, set the milk warming, then leaned against the worktop, gazing at Dax's flowers, still fresh and lovely on the table. Why was she feeling so restless? Why had she spent the last half an hour looking at pictures of Chamonix? Was it because not going meant Chloe was missing out and she was feeling guilty about that, or was it because she couldn't stop thinking about all the things Dax had said in the car?

What was wrong with his mother? Couldn't Colette see that he needed her? Didn't she care about him, or about Yannick, her own grandson? Was she just like André's parents? She felt a cold lump hardening in her stomach. They hadn't helped her either. Instead, two weeks after André's funeral they'd turned on her. Suddenly, she was nothing but a provincial gold-digger who'd trapped André into marriage by getting pregnant! If not for her, he'd have made the Paris Orchestra at twenty-two! If not for her, he'd never have been lumbered with a child, would never have been carrying that child's Christmas present over that crossing! If not for her and Chloe—*Chloe?*—their son would have been alive! She felt tears scalding her eyes, bile stinging her throat. She'd lost it then, torn into them. How dared they implicate her own sweet, innocent girl, the apple of André's eye, their own flesh and blood? How *dared* they? She'd never hated anyone in her life, but she'd hated them then. Still did!

She took a shuddery breath, pushing it all down, feeling sadness flooding in. How could they not love Chloe? How could Colette not want to help Dax with Yann? What kind of people were these?

She closed her eyes, steadying herself. Thank God Maman and Papa weren't like that. They couldn't get enough of their granddaughter. After André died, they'd begged her to go home and for a moment she'd been tempted, but the thing was, she'd have been restless in no time. Paris had always been her dream, and with André gone it had seemed even more important to stay, because it was the city they'd shared, and she wanted Chloe to share it too. Struggling on her own with Chloe had been hard, keeping it from her parents, to stop them worrying, had been hard too, but just knowing that they were there, that she could have cut and run if it had all got too much, had helped her stay strong.

But no one had Dax's back. Colette wasn't

helping, and Amy was leaving. He was all alone, and she couldn't bear the thought of it. When she'd turned down his proposal all she'd seen was his selfishness for wanting to keep riding dangerous lines, but now she was seeing a wider view, a more complicated view. Dax *did* care about Yann. It was why he'd come back to Paris, why he'd put him into a good school. It was why he'd swapped his sexy car for a blue brick, *blue* because Yann liked blue, and it was why he'd pursued her relentlessly to be Yann's childminder for Christmas, because Yann adored Chloe. His instincts, save the one that made him want to throw himself off mountains, were all good. She sighed. But that was the biggie! He *did* want to keep riding down vertical cliffs, and she wasn't fine with it.

She turned back to the stove, opening the hot-chocolate tin. Two scoops for Chloe, not three as it said on the label. Just one of the million things she knew about Chloe, because Chloe was hers, had been hers from that first indignant birth cry. Dax hadn't had that luxury, knowing his son from the beginning. Yann was a stranger. He didn't *love* him yet.

But what if he did?

Would he stop taking risks then?

She stirred in the chocolate, felt her pulse quickening. What if she could help Dax to fall in love with his son? If she went to Chamonix with that express aim, then her conscience could be clear, and Chloe could have her magical Christmas in the mountains with her best friend! Skiing! Dog sledding. All the things Dax had talked about. It was nothing less than she deserved, some proper fun, some happy indulgence. And the money would be such a boost. Enough to furnish their new place when they got it, enough to create a fairy-tale bedroom for Chloe? If she drove a hard bargain, Dax would think she was only going for the money.

'Maman! Look!'

She startled then turned, catching her breath. Chloe was holding up her drawing: snowy mountains cloaked in snowy pines and a little boxy house. She felt a smile loosening her cheeks. 'What a beautiful picture!' She turned off the hob and went over, cupping Chloe's face in her hands. 'Would you like to go to a place like that for Christmas?'

Chloe's face stretched. 'Could we?'

She felt her smile widening, a bubble of happiness exploding in her chest. 'You know, I think it could be arranged...'

CHAPTER FIVE

December 12th, Charles De Gaulle Airport...

'YOU'VE LOST WHO?' Dax was bending down, looking into Yann's face.

Lost? The last word any parent wanted to hear in the middle of a busy airport! She tightened her grip on Chloe's hand, looking Yann over: boots, jeans, blue jacket, orange backpack and... empty hands. *Uh-oh!*

She touched Dax's shoulder. 'He's lost Maurice.'

Dax looked up blankly. 'Who's Maurice?'

Chloe sighed dramatically. 'His bear!'

She touched Chloe's head. 'Dax knows that.' She widened her eyes at him. 'You just forgot for a moment, didn't you, because you're excited about Christmas?'

He blinked, then seemed to catch on. 'That's right. I forgot because I'm stoked for Santa!' He turned back to Yannick. 'So you've lost your teddy...?'

Oh, no!

Yannick bit his lip. 'He's a *panda*!'

Dax's face stretched then tightened.

She pressed her lips together. Hopefully, he was giving himself a roasting! One, for not knowing who and what Maurice was, and two, for not tying Maurice to Yann's backpack as she'd done with Chloe's monkey. She let go of Chloe's hand, dropping down so she could look Yann in the eye. 'That's what Papa meant! Pandas are just black and white teddy bears.' Yann's eyes were glistening, and his bottom lip was trembling. *Oh, God!* She wrapped her hands around his, trying to sound breezy and confident. 'Don't worry.' She flicked a glance at Dax. 'Your *papa* will find Maurice. He's a superhero!'

Yannick looked at Dax balefully.

She held in a sigh. Maybe it was a hard sell, but bigging Dax up to Yann was her job now, part of her plan to zip them together, but that plan was going to be all for nothing if they didn't find Maurice.

Think!

Yann had definitely had Maurice at check-in because while Dax had been hefting their luggage onto the conveyor, a smiling flight attendant had attached a 'special' label to his paw. They'd stopped on the way through Duty Free so that Chloe could examine a tower filled with rainbow sweets, then they'd gone for breakfast. *Bingo!*

She straightened. 'I think he might be—'

'On the bench in the café!' Dax was already shrugging off his pack, dropping it at her feet and then he looked at Yann. 'I *will* find him! I promise.' His eyes snapped to hers. 'Stay right here!' And then he was off, haring through the crowd.

She wedged his bag between her feet. This wasn't a good start! *How* hadn't Dax known who Maurice was? Maybe it really *was* excitement. He certainly seemed to have been high as a kite from the moment she'd said yes. His breath hadn't even hitched when she'd named her price. He'd taken her bank details then asked how soon he could meet Chloe. Would going out for crepes after school the next day suit them?

'Perfect!'

Then, all weekend, gifts had kept arriving. Pink bugaboo pants for Chloe to match her pink jacket. Gloves. Goggles! Several hats. And for her, smart black ski pants and an exquisite red goose-down jacket. *'Expenses!'* And he'd kept calling. Would flying on the twelfth suit her? What did Chloe like to eat, aside from crepes smothered in chocolate? What, aside from flan, did *she* like to eat? Any allergies? Did Chloe prefer duck-down or goose-down pillows? Did she have a preference herself? When Dax had said he was naturally energetic, he hadn't been understating it. He was frenetic. *Kinetic!* Big on detail, and yet for some reason he hadn't known about Maurice!

She looked at the kids. Chloe was comforting Yann, talking to him in low, earnest tones. Chloe was all heart. She'd let Dax in right away, giggling at his jokes in the creperie, teasing him back when he'd teased her. Even Yann had looked on with interest. That was Chloe's gift, shining for everyone, but it had tugged a bit, seeing her shining so readily for Dax. Simone sighed. She'd tried so hard to keep André alive for Chloe, but Chloe was forgetting. These days, when she started telling Chloe how much André had loved the Louvre, how they'd met in front of the Mona Lisa, Chloe always said, *'Maman, I already know the story of you and Papa.'* For Chloe, André was an old story and Dax was a new one, a handsome, charming one, with a melting gaze and heart-stopping smile. Dax was alive. Vital. *Gorgeous!* No wonder Chloe was smitten… But better that than not, right, since they were all going to be spending Christmas together?

The speaker blared suddenly. 'This is the final

call for flight AF1842 to Geneva. Would all passengers please go to the gate immediately?'

'Maman!' Chloe's eyes flew wide. 'That's Geneva! Are we going to miss it?'

Yannick was twisting his hands together, chewing his lips.

Oh, God! What *had* she got herself into? In her head, she'd imagined herself as Mary Poppins, snapping her fingers, oiling the wheels, but the wheels were wobbling, about to come off.

She plastered on a smile, putting a hand on each of their shoulders. 'No! Of course not. The announcements always sound dramatic, but they're used to people running late. They won't go without us.' She swallowed hard. If only that were true. If they didn't get to the gate soon, they wouldn't be allowed to board and then Yann would fall apart completely.

She rocked up onto her toes, heart going, scanning the crowd, and then a face flashed, a mop of dark hair. She locked on just to be sure. It *was* him! Relief streamed through her veins. Dax was sprinting towards them, dodging suitcases, and then his hand went up, and there was Maurice, looking like a crowd surfer, his label flying and spinning.

She felt her heart melting, a smile breaking her face apart. 'Look!' She squeezed Yannick's shoulder, hearing the excitement in her own voice. 'Papa's coming, and he's got Maurice! I told you he was a superhero!'

She took two sweets out of her bag and rose up, stretching across the aisle to hand them over. 'Kids? Suck these and they'll help your ears pop when we take off.'

Yann's face brightened, his cheeks suddenly bursting into Dax's irresistible smile. 'Pop, pop, pop!'

Chloe locked eyes with him, giggling. 'Pop-a-poodle-poo.'

Simone felt a smile coming. Yann was okay. *Happy!* Everything was fine. She dropped back into her seat.

'You're amazing!' Dax's eyes were full of admiration. 'You brought sweets.' His voice dropped to a whisper. 'And you made Yann smile!'

She felt her cheeks flushing. 'Thanks, but I'm not amazing, just well-practised, and, for the record, sweets and smiles tend to go hand in hand.' She stowed her bag, then fished for the two halves of her safety belt, taking her time. Sitting with Dax hadn't been the plan, but the kids had dived into the window seats, begging to sit together, and after all the shenanigans with Maurice they hadn't had the heart to say no. So now she was beside him, breathing in his cologne, trying not to melt every time he looked at her. At least the seats in business class were nice and wide!

'Sim...' He was leaning in, his voice low. 'You think I'm terrible for not knowing about Maurice, don't you?'

What to say? After all his heroics, she'd resolved to keep her thoughts to herself, but if he wanted to know her feelings, she wasn't going to lie. She turned to look at him, keeping her voice low too. 'I don't think you're terrible exactly, but at the same time—'

'There *is* a reason.' His eyes were holding her fast.

She felt a tingle travelling along her spine. Being this close felt rather intimate, but he clearly didn't want Yann overhearing. She swallowed. 'Okay. Go on.'

'Before I went to collect Yann from Tunis, I bought him some toys...' He paused. 'I probably went a bit overboard.'

That fitted! Flowers, clothes, plumbers. The hat off his head! Dax was nothing if not generous. *Kind!*

He shrugged a bit. 'I didn't know what to get. I asked Colette what I'd liked at Yann's age, but she didn't know so I basically bought the shop, including a menagerie of soft toys. Bears, rabbits, tigers, owls. A giant penguin! I put them all on his bed. So many eyes.' He pulled a mock terrified face. 'Staring!'

He was trying to make her smile, but she felt like crying. Lulu the rag doll, Jumpy the rabbit and Serge the monkey would be burned on her memory for ever because Chloe loved them. They were family! But Colette couldn't remember what Dax had used to like! Was that hands-off parenting? No wonder Dax didn't call her Maman.

He shook his head. 'I thought I was going to be like one of those movie dads, you know, propped against the headboard reading bed-time stories, but Yann didn't want me there.' He blinked and then his gaze tightened on hers. 'I didn't push it because I didn't want to cause him stress or make him unhappy. I figured he'd been through enough already. So I stayed out of his room, left bedtimes to Amy, and that's why I didn't know about Maurice.'

She felt her heart going out to him. Yann had shut him out. None of this was his fault. She took a breath, going for the silver lining. 'Well, you do now.'

He nodded. 'I do, and we're never losing him again because next time I'm going to chain him to Yann's bag, like you did with Chloe's monkey.'

He looked so serious that she couldn't help smiling. 'His name is Serge.'

'Serge the monkey...' He tapped his forehead. 'I'm locking it in. One day, you'll be proud of me!'

He was smiling but there was steel in his eyes. He was trying so hard, had been trying right from the start, smothering Yann with toys, expecting to get love back. It wasn't the way things worked, but he deserved Yann's love, he really did, because *his* heart was in the right place. More or less. Free riding aside...

Suddenly she couldn't stop herself from reaching for his hand, wrapping it in hers. 'How do you think I learned to tie Serge to Chloe's bag?'

For a beat he looked startled, probably because she was gripping his hand so hard, but then bemusement lit his eyes. 'I'm guessing maybe Serge got lost...'

'Lost?' She felt laughter bubbling up inside. 'Serge is a specialist. He's been lost in the shoe shop, the dry-cleaners, nursery school twice, the Square des Batignolles more times than I can remember, the Louvre and, ironically, the zoo. *That's* how many times I made the mistake of *not* tying him on, so please, don't ever tell me I'm amazing, or put me on a pedestal.'

His eyes flickered, and then she felt his hands

moving, wrapping around hers, squeezing gently, making her feel all warm and tingly. 'It's too late for that, but you've made me feel a whole lot better about Maurice.'

'Dax's turn!'

He glanced into the rear-view mirror. Chloe was twinkling at him. Yann was smiling too. Maybe not *at him* exactly, but smiling all the same, joining in with the game, and talking, *actually* talking. Hallelujah!

He shot Simone a sideways glance. She was smiling too, her eyes warm. She seemed different, more animated, more…accessible. Maybe it was chatting on the plane—explaining about Maurice, hearing her funny story about Serge— that had softened the air between them. And there'd been her hands too, around his, then his around hers, that feeling of, what? Affection? Connection? Whatever it was, it was still there, flowing back and forth, doing strange things to his pulse.

He turned back to the road. Had she really changed her mind for the five months' salary plus expenses she'd asked for? Not that it mattered. The main thing was, she was here— thank God—making things flow, keeping Yann happy, keeping them all entertained. She'd got them playing a memory game, packing an imaginary suitcase with their favourite things. *Clever!* It meant they were all learning more about each other.

He adjusted his hands on the wheel. 'Okay, I'm going to Chamonix and I'm taking Serge the monkey, Maurice the panda...' He flicked a glance at Simone. 'My piece of flan, my snowboard, my pink woolly hat with the pom pom—'

A sudden throaty chuckle cracked the air. *Yann?* His heart leapt. Was Yann engaging? *With him?* He met Yann's eyes in the mirror, feeling a silly smile breaking his face apart. 'What? Don't you think I'd look nice in pink pom-pom hat?'

Yann clamped his lips together and shook his head, but his eyes were smiling.

Smiling eyes, proper eye contact! His heart leapt again. Milestone moment!

'You're cheating.' Simone was raising her eyebrows at him. 'You're buying time.' But she was messaging him too, with her eyes, telling him that she was seeing everything, feeling happy for him.

He felt another silly grin coming. 'No, I'm not! I'm simply responding to some oblique heckling from the back seat.' Her mouth quirked, sweet, and supremely kissable. He tore his eyes away, focusing on the road. 'Now, where was I? Pink hat, my *crôque monsieur*...'

Funny that Yannick loved that; it was *his* favourite too! 'My...' he looked at Simone '...violin.' She nodded tightly. She played? So many things he didn't know about her and wanted to... *Focus!* 'And—' suddenly he couldn't resist hinting at the surprise he'd planned '—and my Christmas tree!'

'You haven't got a Christmas tree in your suitcase!'

He held in a smile. He'd expected this, Chloe jumping right in. She'd been the same in the creperie, teasing him, but letting him in at the same time. She was adorable, just like her mother. He took a breath, squinting at her through the rear-view mirror. 'How do you know?'

She pouted. 'Because it wouldn't fit!'

'It does because it's a magic Christmas tree.'

Her mouth stiffened and then her face scrunched up. 'You haven't got a magic Christmas tree...'

He looked ahead, feeling her eyes on him, and Yann's, and Simone's, feeling his belly starting to vibrate. Two days ago, he'd hired a team of stylists to deck the chalet. He'd given them his ideas for the Christmas tree, told them to go large with it, create something that would make the kids' eyes pop! When he'd phoned his housekeeper, Chantal, that morning, to see how it was looking, she'd said it was magical! Hence 'magic' Christmas tree! Its magic was already working, sending festive tingles up and down his spine, or maybe he was tingling simply because he was going home, taking Yann to the place he loved most in the world, the place he belonged!

He felt his glow fading suddenly, a band tightening around his chest. Why had he gone back to Paris? Some misshapen instinct? Or panic, pure and simple. Whatever, he should have known better than to run to Colette because Colette had never been what he'd needed her to be. Her love, if that was what it was, had always felt insubstantial, loose around the edges. She'd always seemed more interested in her parties and trips than in him. She'd always let him do exactly what he wanted. At fourteen, what he'd wanted was to spend his days at the skatepark practising fakies, carving and grinding and getting air, enough air to hone his spins and grabs. He'd used to go off in the morning—*to school*—with his skateboard strapped to his pack, but she'd never said a word, never told him to stop playing hooky. She'd just kept on paying the exorbitant school fees. If she hadn't paid for his skateboard and helmet and shin pads too, he'd have wondered if she cared at all.

He looked at Yann in the rear-view mirror. His son was never going to have to wonder if he cared. Yann was going to know it one hundred per cent, even if the only way he could show him right now was with a bonkers Christmas tree. He looked at Chloe. Her little face was still taut, her eyes full of challenge. He felt the magic kindling again, his belly vibrating but laughing would give the game away. He tightened the corners of his mouth, flashing his eyebrows at her in the mirror. 'Well, Chloe, what can I say? You'll just have to wait and see.'

'Fifty-five, fifty-six, fifty-seven...' Simone paused for a beat, trying to keep her face straight. Was she really standing in the entrance lobby of the most gorgeous mountain chalet she'd ever seen, counting to sixty with pair of excited six-year-olds? Dax was inside, taking the 'magic' Christmas tree out of his bag. He'd said he'd need a minute, then they could go in. A ruse obviously, but it was completely impossible not to feel caught up in it. She took a breath, eyeing Chloe and Yann in turn, eking out the last seconds for effect. 'Fifty-eight... fifty-nine...*sixty*!'

The kids dived for the door, pushing it open, then froze. Her jaw went slack. Dax's tree was enormous, filling the stairwell and rising all the way to the galleried landing above. It was dense with silver and burgundy baubles, knobbly brown pinecones and…hundreds of felt animals. She felt a smile curving on her lips. Cheeky rabbits and bushy squirrels, cute mice and bespectacled badgers, wise owls, and wily foxes. A whole woodland carnival!

The kids unfroze suddenly and rushed over, peering into the branches, oohing and ahing.

She looked at Dax. He was watching them, eyes shining, a smile hanging on his lips. Warmth filled her chest. He'd organised this perfect Christmas tree on top of everything else! On the plane, he'd said to her that she was amazing, but *he* was amazing. Kind, thoughtful, good fun and, at that moment, the perfect father.

Suddenly his gaze shifted, catching her. For a moment she couldn't breathe, and then he smiled, and she couldn't breathe all over again. And then he motioned to the floor with a small nod of his head. She looked, stifling a giggle. His holdall was lying open, a length of organza ribbon trailing from its gaping zip, a scatter of pinecones, and woodland creatures, and baubles leading to the base of the tree.

Genius!

'So is this *really* a magic tree!' Chloe was nailing Dax with a look.

'Of course.' He was deadpanning like a pro. 'Did you think I was telling tall tales?'

Chloe's eyebrows knitted. It was her *I'm not sure* face. Dax needed a co-conspirator fast!

She went over, examining the tip of a branch detective-style. 'I have to say, I almost didn't believe it, but—' she turned to Chloe and Yann '—it was clearly a messy business getting it out.'

Chloe and Yann looked at the floor around Dax's bag, then exchanged deep looks.

She sensed Dax smothering a laugh but in the next instant he was dropping down, poker-faced.

'It was. I'm going to need some help tidying up.'

Chloe and Yann hesitated for a nanosecond then they were on it.

She stepped back. Dax needed this time, this kind of interaction with the kids, *with Yann*. He was doing fine, pointing to gaps, helping them hook things back on. Yann was watching Chloe, copying her, but he was also watching Dax. Was he seeing what she was seeing... a different Dax, a happier, more comfortable Dax? Was Yann getting curious about his *papa*? That was good!

She ran her eyes over the wooden balustrades. She was feeling different too. Maybe it was the warm, festive vibe in the hall, that lovely fresh pine smell and the feeling of home that was making her glow inside, or was it something else? She looked at Dax. Smiling. Merry-eyed. Coming to Chamonix for Chloe's sake, and for Yann's sake, had felt right, but at the airport there'd been a moment when she'd felt the weight of what she was doing, an acute awareness that Dax was an unknown. But then on the plane, exchanging parenting stories, she had started to feel that they were the same, just two people trying to be good parents and messing up sometimes. Holding hands, feeling that anchoring warmth flowing between them, had cemented that feeling. After that everything had felt natural and easy.

'Dax!' A smiling, silver-haired woman was coming through the hall towards them. 'I thought I heard voices.'

'Chantal!' Dax straightened, holding out his arms. 'I've missed you!' He gave her a hug, then stepped back. 'Yann, Chloe, Simone, this is Chantal. She's going to be looking after us while we're here.'

Chantal's gaze was warm. 'It's lovely to meet you all.' She turned to Dax. 'Lunch is ready when you are. Are you showing round first, or do you want to eat?'

'What do you think, Simone?' Dax's eyes came to hers. 'Eating or exploring?'

She glanced at the kids. Hopping like frogs!

They wouldn't settle until they'd looked round, and neither would she. The modern stone and timber exterior had taken her breath away as they'd driven up and she was dying to see the rest.

She smiled. 'Exploring!'

CHAPTER SIX

Later...

SIMONE SANK ONTO the bed and blew out a long breath. Putting Yann and Chloe to bed had been easier than she'd thought. She'd suggested to Dax that they read the bedtime story together and he'd been all for it, so they'd planted the kids in Chloe's bed and sat shoulder to shoulder, doing Goody the Elf and Big Bad Giant, Dax trying to rumble his part menacingly but mostly laughing. And then miraculously eyelids had started to droop and that had been that. Dax had taken Yann to his own room while she'd been tucking Chloe in, and moments later he'd reappeared, smiling, saying that Yann had gone out like a light!

It was a good sign, surely? A sign that Yann was relaxed about being here.

She got up and went over to her suitcase, taking things out, putting them in drawers. Some-

thing was definitely happening with Yann. All
through dinner he'd kept shooting glances at
Dax, and Dax had noticed. She'd seen it in his
eyes every time they'd caught hers across the
table. Maybe Chloe's easiness around Dax was
reassuring Yann, making him see his *papa* dif-
ferently, or maybe he was simply mesmerised
because from the moment they'd come through
the door, Dax had been all smiles.

He'd toured them round the house with de-
light strapped to his face. No wonder! His home
was delightful, *no*, breathtaking! Large, light
rooms. Vaulted timber ceilings. Polished wood
floors. Stunning views! The kids had loved
the TV den with its squishy sofas and cinema-
sized screen. She'd loved the immense black
and white photograph of Mont Blanc that covered a whole wall in his office, although she'd
felt trembly too, looking at it, remembering his
film, a speck of Dax on the vast white slope.

In the basement garage he'd shown them his
snowmobile, and his camper van, and the four-
by-four that was hers to drive, but it was his kit
room that had really blown her away. So much
gear! Regiments of snowboards, helmets, boots,
goggles, and bindings, innumerable impeccable
skeins of climbing rope hanging from dozens
of pegs. Ice axes, harnesses, packs, and jackets,
all tidily arranged. He kept the small stuff like

karabiners in neatly labelled colour-coded plastic boxes. *Colour-coded!*

He'd said before that free riding was quite involved but seeing all his kit had brought home how technical it really was. He seemed so knowledgeable, and he was a total neat freak! He'd said keeping tabs on his gear was vital, maintaining it essential. It was reassuring in a way and yet there was that little knot tightening again.

All afternoon, he'd been on the phone, making plans. She'd heard him as she'd been unpacking the kids' things in their rooms. Later, when she'd been in the den watching a silly movie with Chloe and Yann, he'd still been walking around, phone in hand, talking excitedly. Dax was thrilled to be home, definitely, but that wasn't the only reason he was shining like the North Star. He was shining because he was going back out on the mountain, free riding…

Taking risks!

Just the thought of it was making her feel sick, sick for Yann, and—*admit it*—sick for herself. She zipped up her empty suitcase and stood, staring at it. Twelve hours with Dax and she was already in a tangle. Holding hands on the plane, conspiring over the magic tree, playing Goody the Elf to his Big Bad Giant, feeling the hard swell of his shoulder against hers, laughing into his eyes. There was something irresistible about Dax, something that had flipped her over from the very first moment. He had a way of looking at her that made the floor slide, a way of looking at her that made her want something for herself…closeness, connection, the warm touch of someone who wasn't her daughter, but Dax couldn't be that someone. Whilst he was taking risks, the price of caring about him would be always waiting for *that* visit. Grim faces at the door, grim words coming out, that boneless feeling, lungs too tight to breathe, lungs so tight she'd thought she was dying too. She swallowed hard. She'd been through it once, and once was enough. Never again!

If only she could persuade him to stop taking risks, but she'd burned those boats the second she'd 'changed her mind' for money! And now she was here, enjoying his home and his company, getting her wires crossed and her feelings tangled. She had to draw a line somehow, compartmentalise! She was here to give Chloe an amazing Christmas, and she was here to bring Dax closer to Yann. If she succeeded, then hopefully, for the love of his son, he'd stop hurling himself off mountains. And that was it! She took a deep breath. Chloe and Yann *had* to be her sole focus. Making room for her own confusion wasn't an option!

Air! That was what she needed. To clear her head. She grabbed her cardigan, pulling it on as she slid the door open and stepped out onto the veranda. Dax had said that the mountains at dawn were 'sick' but these mountains, vast and ghostly under the stars, were 'sick' too. She leaned against the rail, breathing cold crisp air, listening to the singing silence, and then suddenly, her stomach dipped. Focusing on Yann and Chloe was all very well but they were in bed now. The rest of the evening stretched. Just her and Dax! Alone! And not just *this* evening, but every evening for the next three weeks! She tugged her cardigan tight, heart drumming. How come she was only realising this now? Saying yes, going for crepes, packing, taking Dax's endless calls… Things had moved so fast, she hadn't quite realised… A shiver forked through her shins. She huddled into her cardigan, jiggling. It was too cold to stand around but going inside would mean going downstairs and going downstairs would mean being alone with Dax, trying to stop her senses swimming every time he looked at her, every time he smiled…

She looked along the veranda. It wrapped all the way around the house under cover of the eaves, so the boards were dry and free of snow. Walking always helped, made her feel better. She set off, treading lightly past Chloe's window, and Yann's, then stepping out a bit, breathing deeply. This wasn't so bad. A teeth-chattering stretch in the freezing cold was just what she needed!

She turned the corner, loosening up. The rooms at this side of the house were empty guest rooms so there was no one to disturb. Such a big house for one person or…not! Dax had said he'd built a big place because he was always having friends to stay, free-riding buddies from around the world. It was what they did, hosting each other in one another's homes, spending their evenings planning adventures, looking for new lines.

Dangerous lines!

She swallowed hard. Knotting herself up was pointless. What she needed were strategies to fast-track the father-son bonding process, like… maybe getting Dax to do the bedtime story on his own next time and…maybe finding something that Dax and Yann both liked, something they could do together when Dax got in from the slopes. *Anything* to get them interacting!

She swung around the next corner and stopped dead. The swimming pool below was lit up and glowing like a turquoise jewel, and Dax was front crawling across it at speed, biceps glistening, his hair darkly plastered to his head. He flipped over, then he was coming towards her, arm over arm, head down. She felt the deck sliding under her feet, a sudden thick heat pulsing in her veins. He looked wonderful gliding through the water. She took a breath, tiptoeing nearer, then stopped. What was she doing? Being ridiculous was what! She took a step back, faltering. He was turning again, arrowing through the water, breaking the surface, water streaming off his shoulders and powerful arms. She swallowed a dry edge in her throat. It was impossible not to watch. He was poetry in motion, so graceful, so fast. She went forward again on slow soft feet. As long as he didn't look up… But what if he did? *Oh, God!* What was wrong with her? She was a grown woman, a mother and, at that very moment, his employee! She shrank into her cardigan, heart pounding. She couldn't *be* like this, couldn't let herself get tangled up in the thought of him. She'd told herself that just two minutes ago! He was just a man, swimming in a pool, and she was acting like a schoolgirl with a crush. *Enough!* She needed to say hello then walk on.

She drew a breath and went to the rail. He was midway through another length but then he turned onto his back, floating, staring upwards. She opened her mouth to speak, but suddenly he was turning his head in her direction and then his eyes found hers.

'Hey!' He broke into a smile that cost her a heartbeat. 'Are you coming in?'

'No way! It's freezing!' She rubbed her arms, trying to sound casual. 'I was just taking a walk.'

His feet disappeared then he was rising out of the water, pushing his hair back, his gaze unswerving. 'It *is* heated...'

Was he trying to persuade her? No matter. Talking to him, feeling the warmth in his eyes and his smile was way better than spying on him. She felt a smile unfurling. 'The pool might be, but the air isn't.'

'It's refreshing!' He sank to his chin, tilting his head back. 'Night swimming is the best. Just look at those stars!'

She looked up. 'Strangely enough they look amazing from here too!'

He grinned. 'Fair play, but you *should* try night swimming sometime, or—' he was rising out of the water again, torso glistening '—maybe you'd prefer the hot tub!' He flashed his eyebrows suggestively.

She held in a smile. He was playing with her, flirting for fun. She couldn't resist flirting back. She pulled a lock of hair forward, twisting it in her fingers. 'Ooh... Hot tub? Now you're talking.'

He laughed, then his gaze steadied, holding

her fast. 'If you're not coming in, you should go inside. It's too cold for just a cardigan—'

She arched her eyebrows. 'But a swimsuit's fine?'

His eyes lit. 'Go! Before you catch a cold! I've got ten lengths to go then I'm done.' He dropped down into the water. 'What would you say to us warming up with a cognac in about twenty minutes?'

She could hardly say no and she didn't want to. She smiled. 'I'd say that sounds perfect!'

CHAPTER SEVEN

Twenty minutes later...

DAX POURED COGNAC into two glasses, then pushed the cork back into the bottle slowly. Fifty laps of the pool should have taken the edge off his jitters, but his stomach was still twisting itself into knots. Crazy! It wasn't as if he wasn't looking forward to spending the evening with Simone. He absolutely was.

He liked her, liked the way he felt inside whenever her eyes held him, liked the way her lips curved up so sweetly when she smiled. Maybe that was the problem! He liked her *too* much. She was stirring things inside him that he didn't recognise, things he didn't know how to process. Reading the bedtime story had tipped him over the edge. Feeling her shoulder against his, the small movements of her body, her warmth. He could have leaned away but something had kept him there, something he hadn't been able to control. He'd tried to swim it off but, somehow, suddenly she'd been there, smiling down at him, heating his blood all over again.

He blew out a breath. When Simone had said yes to Chamonix, it had felt like a chance for him to get his life under control again, but it wasn't feeling like that any more. It was so good to be home, but it wasn't the same. *He* wasn't the same. Yes, he'd felt the same old excitement talking on the phone to his free-riding buddies, making plans for getting out on the slopes, but he'd also felt as if he was missing out on what Simone and the kids were doing, missing out on their laughter and happy chatter. He'd wandered around the house, talking on the hoof, just to see them, just to catch traces of Simone's perfume in the air...

His chest went tight. A feeling of home and family was what he'd wanted for Yann, to make him happy. It was why he'd begged Simone and Chloe to come but getting caught up in it himself was the last thing he'd expected. He didn't know what it meant, or how to feel about it. It was like dangling, mid-somersault, not knowing what the landing was going to be like, and feeling hopelessly attracted to Simone wasn't helping things, especially since there was something in her eyes that was making him think she liked him too.

He picked up the glasses and started walking. She was in the sitting room waiting for him, stunning in grey jeans and a soft black shirt, her hair loose for once and hanging darkly around her lovely face. He broke step, drawing in a steadying breath. She was lovely. He liked her in all the ways it was possible to like someone, but she was here for Yannick, and no way could he risk Yann's happiness, Yann's Christmas, by making a stupid move on her. It had been hard enough persuading her to come in the first place.

'I'm seeing a change in Yann.' Simone was dropping onto the opposite sofa, settling her glass on her knee. He felt his tension melting away. Talking about Yann would pull him out of his own head. Besides, he was keen to hear her thoughts. She smiled, 'I mean the way he's watching you all the time. I think it's a good sign.'

'I hope so.' Yann had definitely been watching him more, making eye contact. He'd even seen glimmers of interest. Yann still wasn't talking to him much, but he'd let him tuck him into bed easily enough. It was progress, and if Simone was seeing it too, then it had to be real. He felt a sudden swell of gratitude. If he'd been on his own with Yann, it wouldn't have been happening. He shifted, stretching out his legs. 'I think Chloe's a big influence.'

She smiled, her eyes flickering with just a hint of mischief. 'Just as well she's on your side!'

'True!' He chuckled. Chloe was definitely on his side. She was something else! He sipped his cognac, suddenly wanting to let some of what he was holding inside come out. 'Chloe's a beautiful soul, Sim. She's like you...' Something flickered behind her gaze. Was he overstepping? It wasn't his intention. He just wanted her to know how grateful he was that she'd come through for him. Maybe a little humour would help. He smiled. 'She's kind, blisteringly honest, and willing to give a hopeless loser like me a chance.'

She blinked. 'Thank you! I think.' She sipped her drink, and then a spark lit her gaze. 'And you're not a *hopeless* loser. You're good at losing panda bears...'

He grinned. 'Like I said, blisteringly honest!'

She laughed softly for a moment and then her eyes became serious. 'Can I be blisteringly honest now?'

His heart panged, not out of fear but out of curiosity. He trusted her. Anything she had to say was worth hearing. He nodded. 'Of course.'

She drew up her legs, tucking them under. 'I

think you should talk to Yann about his mother.' His heart panged again, this time with guilt and a confusion of other emotions that he couldn't quite pin down. 'I understand why you went for the fresh start, but you can't just wipe people away like that, not a mother, not a father, not if they've been loved…' The corners of her eyes were glistening. 'Yann's grieving. You need to open a door for him so he knows he can talk about her if he wants to.'

'But how?' He felt a wave of hopelessness. 'I only knew Zara for a couple of weeks, and we didn't exactly spend our time talking.'

'There must be something?' Her gaze was gentle, urgent.

'I don't…' He sipped his cognac, thinking. 'She was quite a bit older than me, ran her own business, Desert Jeep Adventures. It's how we met.' His chest went tight. 'It's how she died actually…rolled a jeep…knocked her head.'

Simone's hand flew to her chest. 'God… that's…'

'I know.' He swallowed hard. 'Anyway, I was on one of her tours. She knew the desert, knew the best parasailing places. That was her thing—parasailing. She was good on a horse too.' He felt a smile coming. 'She was action girl! A free spirit. She had these amazing amber eyes…'

'Did you love her at all?' Simone's gaze was hopeful.

'No.' What would she say if he told her that he'd never been in love, didn't know what it felt like?

'Right.' She drew in a little breath. 'Well... you could tell Yann how you met Zara...tell him that you thought her eyes were amazing. Share everything you have because Zara's your bridge. *Use* her, and let Yann *use* her too. Let him remember her through you.' Her eyes were glistening again. 'You need to keep her alive for him.'

He could feel her passion, see it blazing in her eyes. She was right. *Wise!* Zara was the path he should have followed from the start. Why hadn't he? He looked down, swirling his cognac, losing himself in its amber glow, and suddenly he knew. He hadn't wanted to talk to Yann about Zara because he'd been afraid that Yann would see that he hadn't loved her. Maybe Yann wouldn't have cared; maybe Zara had told him already, but what if she hadn't? He hadn't wanted to be the one to reveal the truth, be-cause knowing that your origins weren't rooted in love was the kind of knowledge that gnawed at your soul, made you feel less... The feeling never went away, even if you told yourself that you were being stupid because it didn't matter, even if you told yourself you didn't care—

'Dax!' Her voice pulled him back. 'Are you okay?'

He blinked, saw concern in her eyes. For some reason it warmed him. He dug out a smile. 'Yes. I was just thinking about what you said, thinking that you're always right.'

'Don't say that.' She was shaking her head. 'I'm not always right. I'm only making a suggestion because I see a change in Yann, and it would be so great if you could build on it somehow…and quickly!' Her eyes flashed. '*Carpe diem* and all that!'

He raised his glass to her. 'It's always been my motto!'

'Figures!' Her glass went up too, and then she took a small sip. 'So… You're planning to go free riding tomorrow?'

'Yes.' He felt a buzz starting in his veins. 'Or, actually, no. Not free riding. If the conditions are right, I'm going out, but I'll be sticking to the resorts. I need to ease back in—'

'*Ease* back in?' She was arching her eyebrows playfully.

He grinned. 'Which for me obviously means I'll be tanking it, but it'll just be playing plus a little bit of work. My sponsors have sent me some bindings to test.'

'What do you mean *test*?' The playful light disappeared. 'Don't tell me you're expected to find out if something's going to break?'

'No!' She was jumping for the wrong stick! He drew in his legs and sat forwards. 'I don't test equipment to see if it works. It absolutely does work, okay?' She was biting her lips, holding him in an anxious gaze. He ran his tongue across his lip. This wasn't the moment to be thinking about kissing her worries away. He swallowed. 'It's more of a review, a question of how things feel, and it's subjective, of course. A binding might suit me but not you.' He couldn't resist. 'In the same way that you might prefer flan from one patisserie over another.'

A smile ghosted on her lips, but there were familiar clouds behind her eyes. He felt a knot tightening in his stomach. They hadn't revisited the sticky subject of risk since her outburst in his apartment. He thought she must have put her feelings aside somehow, because she was here, wasn't she? But they were still there after all, frozen into the ice, just visible. It was no good! She was helping him out. She deserved to have a nice Christmas, not one spent tying herself into needless knots. He couldn't bear the thought of that.

He parked his glass on the low coffee table and fastened his eyes on hers. 'Sim, I don't want you being anxious all the time. It's not necessary.'

She blinked, as if she hadn't expected him to be so direct, and then she swallowed, a glimmer of steel in her gaze. 'Why isn't it necessary? I want to know.'

Finally! A chance to lay it all out! He took a breath, feeling the words rising like a tide. 'First, because for me free riding is as natural as walking...or breathing. I do it without having to think about it. Secondly, the film you saw was a grand spectacle, a few high-octane minutes set to music, but you need to stop reacting and look deeper...*think* deeper.' The corners of her mouth started to tighten but her gaze held steady. He licked his lips. 'Look, every line I ride is earned in hours of preparation. I study the terrain from the top and from the bottom. I consult with expert mountaineers. I go on recces. You need to understand that when I'm up there on the mountain, I'm doing things I've done hundreds, thousands of times before. Every jump, every somersault you see has a thousand others behind it. I've been riding snowboards for thirteen years, and before that I was riding skateboards. All in all, it's a lot of practice!'

Something came and went behind her eyes. *Acknowledgement? Understanding?* He pushed on. 'In the beginning I made mistakes, of course

I did, but every mistake is a lesson. You learn. You grow. You get better, but you can never get complacent. The mountain *is* dangerous. You have to give it your full attention, all of your respect, and I do—*always*—so the risk for me is small.'

She lifted her chin. 'Maybe the risk is small, but the consequences of something going wrong are huge, especially now.'

His chest panged. He couldn't argue with that, but he wasn't going to let anything go wrong. He had no intention of orphaning his son and he *needed* her to understand that, needed to see it register in her eyes.

He got up and went to sit beside her. 'You're right. The consequences would be huge, which is exactly why I'm not going to let anything bad happen. I don't want to die! Why would I risk my life when I have so many reasons to live?' Her eyes were on his, full of thoughts he couldn't read. Maybe if he told her the last thing, the thing he'd never told anyone before, it would ease her mind. He took a breath. 'You know, it's strange… I grew up in Paris, but the mountains have always felt like home. It's like they're in my blood. I feel…' How to explain? 'I feel I have a sort of *sense* for the mountain, like a sixth sense. When I'm out there, I can feel if something isn't right, and if it isn't right then I turn back.'

The light in her eyes softened. 'You turn back?'

'Always.' Her eyes were flickering, tugging at something inside him. He swallowed. 'Whatever impression you have of me from that film, the truth is that I'm not remotely reckless. I've never been reckless. I'm—'

'Meticulous!' A smile warmed her eyes. 'That's if your kit room is anything to go by!'

His chest filled. Simone's smile was already one of his all-time favourite views. He shook his head, chuckling. 'Meticulous is a polite way of putting it. I was going to say I'm on the scale when it comes to my mountain adventures.'

She took a sip from her glass then set it down. When she looked up again, her gaze was soft and full. 'So I can trust that your sixth sense is going to keep you safe?'

His heart thumped sideways. Her need for reassurance was turning him inside out. She seemed so vulnerable, so afraid and he couldn't stand it. He wanted to scoop her up, shield her from every terrible thing in the world, but at the same time he wanted to tug her out onto the ledge, show her some thrills, see her cheeks glowing and her eyes shining. More than anything, he wanted her to be happy.

He leaned towards her. 'Yes, you can.' He

touched her hair without thinking, sliding his fingers down one smooth lock. 'I don't want you worrying, okay?'

Her eyes held his for a moment and then she looked down.

Oh, God! He dropped his hand. 'I'm sorry.' He swallowed hard, heart pounding. He hadn't meant to touch her; it had just happened, a tender impulse, a desire to sweep away her worries, and her hair was so lovely, the way it hung at the side of her face, glowing in the firelight. He touched her hand with one finger. 'I'm sorry. I shouldn't have done that... I wasn't trying to—'

'It's okay.' She looked up, blinking, and then her gaze settled. 'The truth is I liked it.' The tip of her tongue flicked across her lip. 'I haven't...' She took a breath, swallowing. 'No one's touched me like that for a long time.'

His heart pulsed. What was she saying? He looked into her face, running his eyes over the curve of her cheek, the soft pout of her lips, then back to her steady gaze and suddenly he knew. She was asking for more, asking him for something he desperately wanted to give.

He leaned towards her again, running the back of his index finger along her cheekbone, watching, giving her a chance to pull away, but she wasn't pulling away. She was leaning into his touch, her eyes hazing over, her lips parting. A voice in his head was saying no, was saying that he was crossing the very line he'd told himself he couldn't cross, but it was a small voice, close to noiseless and then it was gone. He looked at her lips, and then he moved in, taking them slowly, tasting cognac and warmth, feeling his pulse heating, gathering. And then her mouth was softening, moulding to his. She was kissing him back, pulling him closer and suddenly he was free falling, hungrier for her than he'd ever felt for anyone. He cupped her nape, deepening his kiss, exploring the sweet wet heat in her mouth, feeling desire blazing through his veins, feeling her hands in his hair, tugging him closer, deeper, and deeper…and then suddenly it wasn't enough. He broke off, heart pounding, kissing her neck, tasting her throat, moving his hands over the soft silk of her shirt, over her breasts, over her hardening nipples. She gasped, then her body was rising to meet him, and her hands were under his shirt, moving over his skin. It was too much sensation. He wanted her, right there, right then, and her body was telling him she wanted him right back. He went for her buttons but then suddenly she was fighting him off, pushing his hands away, her voice a sort of strangled whisper. 'Dax!'

'What?' He felt dizzy, momentarily blind, his heart pounding broken beats. 'What did I do?'

She was shaking her head. 'It's Yann!'

Yann! He looked round. *Oh, God!* Yann was bumbling towards them. He sprang to his feet, heart banging. Was Yann sick? He hurried across, scanning him from head to toe. He didn't look sick. He was yawning, and sleep rumpled, but still, he was here, wanting something or someone. *Him?* Couldn't be. Yann *never* wanted him.

He swallowed hard. 'Yann? Are you all right?'

Yann rubbed at his eyes, swaying slightly. He seemed so small, seemed as if he should be picked up and held on a hip, but they weren't on tactile terms yet. If he scooped Yann up, he'd probably frighten him half to death. A memory flashed. Simone, eye to eye with Yann at the airport. *Of course.* He dropped to his haunches, taking Yann's shoulders in his hands. 'Are you okay?'

Yann's eyes fastened on his, sleepy but direct. 'I want to see the snowboards.'

Definitely not what he'd been expecting! He licked his lips. 'Which snowboards?'

Yann blinked. 'In the room downstairs. I want to see them.'

His heart pulsed. Yann was interested in snowboards! If only he'd known, he could have talked to him about it before. Why hadn't he? He felt his chest tightening. Because he'd been too busy trying to be a movie dad, and failing, and then he'd backed off altogether. He gulped a breath. Too late to worry about that now! The main thing was, Yann was interested, and *that* opened things up! He felt a sudden rush of euphoria, a silly grin splitting his face apart. 'Of course you can see them—'

'After breakfast in the morning!' Simone was suddenly beside him, a noticeable flush in her cheeks. Her eyes caught his. 'Maybe you could treat us all to a demonstration tomorrow!' She smiled at Yannick. 'You know your *papa*'s pretty sick on a snowboard, huh?'

Sick! It sounded cute coming from her lips.

'Can I have a go?' Yann was winding up, his eyes brightening. 'Please can I have a go, Papa?'

Papa! His ribs went tight. Yann had just looked him in the eye and called him Papa! Was this really happening? He took a breath. He'd intended being on the slopes first thing, loosening up, giving those bindings a spin, but now...? Yann's eyes were gripping his. *Papa!* He felt his pulse going, his thoughts free riding a hundred lines at once. He could spend time with Yann first thing, couldn't he, give them all a demonstration before going to the resort? Then, he could stop in Cham on the way back, pick up a junior board for Yann, and one for Chloe too. Or maybe Simone and the kids could meet him in town. Even better! He could show them around, the kids could choose their own boards, and after, they could go for hot chocolate, soak up the Christmas vibes…

He squeezed Yann's shoulders gently. 'Of course you can, but my board's going to be too big. We'll have to get you your own.'

Yann's eyes popped. 'My *own* board!'

Yann was adorable. He really was!

He felt a smile breaking over his face again. 'Hell yeah! A serious snowboarder needs his own board!'

'But—' Simone was interrupting again '—serious snowboarders also need a good night's sleep, don't they, Dax?'

He twisted to look up at her, losing himself in the warmth of her gaze, hoping she could feel his gratitude flowing back. She was keeping him on track, reminding him that buying Yann a board was the easy part! Taking Yann back to bed, making sure he understood rules and boundaries, was harder. He felt a bitter pang in his chest. Colette had mobbed him with things, but she'd never said no to him, never given him the security of boundaries, even though he'd pushed and pushed. She'd made him feel that he didn't matter, that he wasn't worth caring about. He was never going to let Yann feel like that.

He turned back to Yann, straightening. 'Simone's right. Snowboarding is super physical, so you need your sleep.' Yann was looking up at him, seeming to take it all in. He felt a small flush of triumph. He steered Yann round slowly, propelling him gently towards the door. 'Let's get you back into bed. Maurice will be wondering where you are.'

'No, he won't.' Yann walked steadily, his small bare feet thudding softly on the floor. 'Maurice can't wonder things. He's just a cuddly toy.'

She watched them go, heart hammering. Had Yann seen? It didn't seem like it, but it had been a close shave.

Oh, God!

She went back to the sofa and picked up her glass, slugging down the last mouthful. But he could have! And then what? Disaster! She felt the cognac burning, her stomach rolling and churning. She set the glass down and pressed her fingers to her temples. What had she been thinking? She'd taken a tender moment and spun it into something else, lost control of her emotions because for a tantalising moment Dax had made her feel that it was safe to like him, because he was safe on the mountain…

Everything he'd said had made sense. About his films being showcases for the skills he'd been honing and practising for years. It had struck her that it was the same with playing the violin. When she played, she was playing more than the music. She was playing every second, every minute, every hour she'd ever played. It was all there underneath, like a huge well that rose up, powering her fingers, pouring through her. That was what Dax had, a wealth of knowledge and experience behind him and…a sense for the mountain. A sixth sense! She got that too because she'd always had a sense for music, a connection to it that she couldn't explain. It was simply there.

She stared at the fire letting the flames blur. He'd said he always turned back if it didn't feel right. He'd said he wasn't reckless. All his reassuring words and all the tidy rows in his kit room had stacked together with the tender look in his eyes, and then he'd touched her hair… She closed her eyes, feeling it again, the gentle slide of his fingers, her limbs melting, desire aching in her veins. That was the moment she should have left alone but couldn't. For three years she'd been swallowing pain and anger, plastering on smiles for Chloe's sake, but when Dax had touched her, she'd felt something warm and real unfolding, too bright and lovely to bury with all the sad bones. She'd wanted more, wanted to lose herself in something that felt good, so she'd opened the door…and he'd stepped through…and his kiss had felt so right, so perfect. Warm, tender, then wild, kindling a fire in her veins, bringing her blazing to life. It was as if everything she'd felt flowing between them from the start had found a place to be, a place that felt like home.

She got up, wrapping her arms across her front. But was it a safe home? Could she risk planting her feelings there, risk letting them grow? After everything he'd said, she felt easier about him going on the mountain, but she'd never be able to switch off her anxiety altogether. And getting closer to him, caring about him would lead Chloe in the same direction, and then what? If something bad did happen, everything would come crashing down. Bad enough for herself, but for Chloe it would be worse. Chloe had barely turned three when André died. She hadn't quite understood, but now Chloe was older, more vulnerable emotionally.

She felt her heart twisting. She couldn't not like Dax. He was warm-hearted and gorgeous. Tormented too. It felt as if they'd been through so much together already, just to get here…the bistro, his presents, that day at his apartment, that car ride back to the school. Maybe that was why her emotions were all over the place, why her feelings were so tangled? She bit her lips together. But she couldn't afford to let herself get tangled, for her own sake and for Chloe's. And there was Yann too.

Yann!

He'd called Dax Papa! He was interested in the snowboards! Good things were happening! Dax had a toehold now and they couldn't jeopardise that, couldn't risk confusing the kids and themselves. Surely, he'd see it too.

'Hey!' Dax was coming towards her, cognac bottle in hand. 'How about a top-up?'

'No, thanks.' Her mouth was dry, but more cognac was the last thing she needed. She watched him pouring a measure into his own glass. What was he thinking about? What was he feeling? Her own nerves were chiming. They'd kissed— more than kissed—and she wanted to talk about it but diving straight in didn't seem right. She needed to ease in somehow. She moistened her lips. 'You must be thrilled about Yann's interest in snowboarding.'

'Just a bit!' He dropped down onto the opposite sofa, shaking his head. 'When he said it, I was like...*what*?'

Was Dax trying to signal something by not sitting beside her? It pricked a bit, but maybe it was also reassuring. If he was distancing himself then maybe he was on the same page about the kiss.

She smiled. 'Well, I think it's great.' In spite of her nerves, she felt a little rush of warmth, a burst of happiness for him. 'It's a way in. It's exactly what you need.'

His hand went up, fingers crossing. 'Here's hoping.'

'I have a good feeling.' She took a breath, feeling her heartbeat pulsing through her skin. 'And...speaking of needs...what you don't need...' His eyebrows drew in slightly. 'What neither of us needs is to be...'

'To be what?' The light in his eyes was fading along with his smile.

Her heart panged. Maybe using the opposite sofa hadn't been a signal. Maybe he'd just been giving her some space. Hadn't he told her before that he liked to think of himself as a gentleman? *Oh, God!* She couldn't not say what she had to say, but she didn't want to hurt him. Maybe if she took it all on her own shoulders it would soften the blow. It was pretty much the shape of things anyway.

She swallowed hard. 'To be making mistakes, to be complicating things for ourselves and the kids.' Something flickered behind his eyes but trying to fathom what it was wasn't an option. She had to keep going. 'Kissing was a mistake,

Dax. I instigated it, and I'm sorry. I wasn't trying to lead you on. I'm just lonely, that's all. And sad…' She felt the truth of it stinging, filling her eyes, then more truths surfacing, wanting to be free. 'I miss being touched, being held. I miss having someone…' A shadow crossed his face and then kindness bloomed in his gaze. She felt it tugging at her, tugging more out of her. 'I lost my husband three years ago… December the seventeenth.'

His eyes narrowed a little. 'I'm sorry.'

For some reason, now she'd started, the words wouldn't stop coming. 'He was just crossing the road…using a crossing…not jaywalking…' She felt a band tightening around her skull. 'The driver was texting…didn't see. André died instantly. That's what they said…'

Suddenly Dax was sitting down next to her, putting his glass into her hands. 'Here.'

'Thanks.' She took a sip, feeling the burn in her throat, feeling the band around her skull tightening. 'I shouldn't be drinking this. I haven't got a head for spirits.' He was looking at her gently, stirring something inside again that she couldn't allow to be stirred. She gave him the glass back. 'It's just a sad time of year, you know. A fragile time. I hide it from Chloe. She doesn't know when her *papa* died, and I'm not going to tell her. I don't want her to be sad.'

'I get that.' Dax shifted a little, and then his eyes came back to hers. 'Just to square things away, what happened isn't on you, Simone. I started it.' His eyes clouded. 'And I shouldn't have. It *was* a mistake, I agree.' His jaw seemed to tighten. 'If Yann had seen—'

'I know.' Her stomach dipped. If Yann had seen, he'd have been confused...troubled... And what if it had been Chloe? *Oh, God!* She drew in a breath. 'I'm glad you feel the same.'

He was nodding. 'One hundred per cent.'

'Good!' She bit her lips, feeling awkward, feeling a sudden tug of weariness. 'If you don't mind, I think I'll go to bed.' She pushed herself up. 'It's been quite a day.'

He was getting up too. 'Simone...?' His gaze was reaching in, turning her over. 'Are we all right?'

'Of course. I'm tired, that's all.' She took a backwards step, suddenly needing not to be trapped in the warm light of his gaze. 'Good-night, Dax.'

CHAPTER EIGHT

December 13th

'DO YOU FEEL SAFE?' Simone was giving Yann a deep look.

Yann nodded, then he twisted his head up, eyes bright, voice revving like an engine. 'I want to go fast, Papa!'

'Really?' Dax felt a smile breaking his face apart. 'I'd never have guessed!'

Yann grinned a devilish grin.

He felt a glow rising inside. *This* was the lively little boy Zara's parents had talked about, the one they couldn't keep up with. Now it made sense! He felt an urge to ruffle Yann's hair but held back. A mistimed paternal gesture might dent things, and he didn't want to do that. Feeling stoked about the way things were going would have to be enough for now.

He tested his feet in his bindings, checking they were tight, then he checked Yann's feet, wedged in the gap between his own. Giving Yann a ride on his snowboard hadn't been part of the plan, but after he'd done his performing seal routine, as per Simone's suggestion last night, Yann had mobbed him, begging for a go. Saying no had been impossible.

He shifted his stance, getting ready, pinning Yann against him.

'Not too fast, Dax, okay?' Simone was looking at him, a trace of the night before in her eyes.

He felt warmth filling his chest then a pang, remembering that he'd agreed with her that their kiss and all the rest had been a mistake. *Agreed!* So there was absolutely no reason for him to be feeling tight around the ribs. It wasn't as if *Mistake!* hadn't been chiming in his ears all the way up the stairs. It was what he'd been thinking as he'd been putting Yann into bed, reflecting on the matter of seconds that had come between himself and disaster, reflecting on the fact that if Yann had seen him tearing off Simone's blouse, they'd never have got onto the subject of snowboards at all!

Tucking Yann in, he'd felt the whole weight of his mistake pressing down on him. Yann had to be his priority. He'd lost his head for a moment, lost himself in Simone's kiss, in the idea of her, but the reality was that he'd never be able to bring her happiness. He didn't do love and commitment. Relationships! He'd dangled on the strings of Colette's changing moods and whims for too many years to ever want to put anyone else through it on his own account. He didn't want anyone's happiness tied to his actions, his mistakes, especially not Simone. She was too lovely, too kind. And…he needed her to be there for Yann.

He'd had it all straight in his head by the time he'd gone downstairs. He'd grabbed the cognac—Dutch courage—and gone in, all set to be open and honest with her, but she'd beaten him to it, started talking about her husband, and Christmas…being lonely…feeling fragile…in a roundabout way telling him that she'd reached for him simply because he'd been there. So that had been that! All tidied up and tucked away, except, for some reason, he could feel a loose thread trailing, catching his feet every time she looked at him.

He threw her a smile, flashing his eyebrows. 'You know me. I *never* go too fast!' And then he rocked the board, making it slide. 'Okay, buddy, here we go…'

'Be careful!' Simone was calling out from the depths of her red jacket, her face luminous in the snow light.

'Sorry?' He put his hand to his ear, just to tease her. 'I didn't quite catch…' and then he had to face forwards because they were picking up speed and Yann was squealing.

He rode a wide arc, holding Yann firm, then wove the other way, keeping the pace easy, the arc gentle. He looked down at Yann's dark head. 'Are you okay?'

'Yes, but I want to go *faster*!'

'No way!'

'Why?'

He held in a smile. 'Because you're loose cargo! You need bindings.' He turned the board sideways, coasting to a sedate stop.

'Is that it?' Yann was looking up at him, his face the picture of disappointment.

He laughed. 'I'm afraid so. We can't go too far because Chloe's waiting for her turn. Besides, we have to walk back, remember.'

'Or you could push me?' Yann's gaze was mischievous. 'That way I get to ride by myself!'

'Okay.' He felt his lips twitching. There were certainly no flies on Yann! 'Hop off a sec.'

Yann jumped into the snow, then strode around, making footprints.

Dax watched while he freed his feet from the bindings. Could this be a Zara moment? Simone had said he needed to talk about her. If only he could think of something that would blend, not sound like he was trying too hard. He sighed.

Maybe something would come, eventually. He straightened the board. 'Right, on you get.'

Yann obeyed, planting his feet wide for balance. 'Let's go!'

It was impossible not to laugh. He fitted his palm between Yann's shoulder blades. 'Brace yourself, okay…'

Yann stiffened then yelled, 'Push!'

He obeyed, chuckling. Yann was no weight at all, going along on the board. His own feet were sinking, but trudging was part of any climb, not that this was a climb, just a gentle upwards slope. He looked ahead, saw Chloe jumping up and down next to a small snow…what? *Rabbit?* Simone's idea no doubt, keeping Chloe busy while she was waiting. Simone was so great at the parenting thing. *So great!* He felt his ribs tightening again. Was it going to happen every time he thought about her, even when it was innocent stuff that had nothing to do with the way her mouth had felt on his, or the way she'd tasted, all cognac and sweetness and something that was just *her*, something that had stripped away his reason and driven him to—?

'Is it my turn now, plee-ee-ase?' Chloe was scampering up with big, excited eyes. Her facial expressions were a hundred per cent Simone, but she must have got her fair hair and blue eyes from André, the man who still owned Simone's heart.

He swallowed hard, shooting her a smile. 'Absolutely. Just let me shed this load first!' He gave Yann a boost then let go.

Yann whooped, riding the glide, then sprang off. Quick as a coin, he flipped himself over, his eyes on fire. 'When I get my own board, I'm going to go like a rocket!'

'No, you won't.' He tried adding a firm little note, Simone-style. 'You'll learn the basics and you'll go slowly to begin with.'

Simone came up. 'Yann, your *papa* is a big expert, remember.' For a beat her eyes met his, all warm. 'If you want to be as good as he is, you need to do what he says.'

'But slow is *so* boring.' Yannick was flapping his arms and legs, making a snow angel.

Snow angel!

'Is it my turn now…plee-ee-ase?' Chloe was tugging his sleeve.

'Chloe! Let Dax catch his breath, please.' The tugging stopped. Simone was raising her eyebrows at Chloe. 'You'll get a turn in a moment.'

Chloe let out a dramatic sigh then dived into the snow next to Yann. 'I made a snow bunny, see, over there.'

'Hey!' Simone was suddenly in front of him,

her voice low but loaded with a smile. 'Things seem to be going well with Yann.'

Because of you. Because you came...

'Yes.' He licked his lips, trying not to look at hers. 'My son seems to have a sense for snow and a passion for speed.'

'It must run in the blood.' She chuckled. 'Like quicksilver!'

'Funny!' His ribs were going again. Something in her eyes was tugging at him, making him want to pull her into his arms and kiss her senseless. *Mistake!* He looked down, steadying himself, noticing her feet. Her boots were damp around the toe. Leaky! That wouldn't do, not at all. He looked up. 'So, last night I had an idea...'

'Oh?'

He could see the words *last night* glitching in her eyes, could feel them glitching in his own. He swallowed hard. 'I was thinking that you and the kids could come with me to Cham. You could have lunch at the resort while I'm on the slopes, then after we could hit town, do some snowboard shopping for the kids, and we need to get you some new boots...'

She seemed to falter, and then she smiled. 'That sounds great, but I don't need new boots.'

'You do! Your feet are wet!'

'They're not wet.' Her cheeks were colouring slightly. 'They're a little damp but it's fine.'

Why did she have to be so stubborn? He shifted stance. 'Please don't fight me. The deal was your fee *plus* expenses, and boots count as expenses. You wouldn't need them if you weren't here.'

'I just…' Something shimmered through her gaze, but he couldn't grasp it, couldn't make sense of it.

What he could sense, at the edge of his vision, was Chloe's pent-up excitement. He couldn't keep her waiting. 'Look, Sim. I *want* to buy you some boots, okay, so please, just let me!'

'All right.' She took a breath and then her gaze filled with warm light. 'You're so kind, Dax.'

He felt his breath catching. Had anyone ever looked at him the way she was looking at him?

'Honestly, it's nothing.' He took a backwards step, collecting himself. 'So, you're sure you're cool with me taking Chloe?'

'Of course…' Her eyebrows slid up. 'But no somersaults!'

'Aww…' He sagged, faking disappointment. 'Really?'

Her face broke apart, and then she was laughing, properly laughing all the way to her eyes. He felt his ribs loosening, his muscles, everything. This was better. The two of them getting on like before… Friends! On the way to being friends anyway, having fun in the snow with the kids on a bright, sunny morning with a great day ahead to look forward to. Looking forward was the thing. They'd made a kissing mistake, but they were pushing past it, moving on, and it was the right thing to be doing. Absolutely the right thing!

He tipped her a wink, then turned. 'Chloe! Are you ready for a ride?'

'*Vin chaud* or hot chocolate?' Dax's gaze was soft and twinkly, his hair rimmed with golden light from the Christmas stalls behind him. It was the same buttery light that was making Chloe's and Yann's faces glow, although the hefty packages under the table—two junior snowboards with boots and bindings—probably had something to do with it too. Early Christmas presents, he'd said.

Carpe diem! That was Dax. Bounding around in the ski shop, pulling out boards, running his fingers over them, scrutinising, then moving on to boots and bindings, checking the fit with the kids, being meticulous! And he didn't forget her boots, the boots that were keeping her toes toasty at that very moment, the boots she'd tried to refuse because for a split second she'd felt overwhelmed by him, overwhelmed that he'd even noticed the slight dampness around her toes when he'd been non-stop turning tricks and taking the kids for snowboard rides.

For a heartbeat, the light in his gaze had felt confusing. It had felt like something to take apart and think about, but then he'd mentioned expenses and she'd come to, remembering that they'd put the previous night behind them, that what they had was a business arrangement, a business arrangement that somehow still seemed to include warm twinkly gazes and snowboarding gear for Chloe. And now his wallet was out again. It was too much! It wasn't as if she didn't have money of her own now, thanks to him.

She reached into her bag. '*Vin chaud*, please, but I'm paying!' She pulled out two notes, offering them over with what she hoped was a firm look.

His head tilted.

'Dax, please…' He was doing that cute thing he did, that one-eye-closed scrunchy-smile thing, building up to a refusal. *Impossible!* She narrowed her eyes at him, trying not to laugh. 'Don't make me come over there.'

He fired a wild-eyed look at Chloe. 'Should I be scared?'

Chloe giggled, then nodded deeply at him. 'Yes. If you don't do what Maman says you'll be in *big* trouble.'

'Well, I definitely don't want to be in *big* trouble!' His eyes came back to hers, holding for a beat as he took the notes, making her breath catch. 'So, it's two deluxe hot chocolates, one *vin chaud*, a coffee and pastries!' He smiled a quick smile, then he was off, see-sawing through the crowd towards the hot-chocolate stalls.

She watched him disappearing, feeling all kinds of tingles. Warm ones for the way he'd been with the kids that morning. Grateful ones for his kindness over her boots and for getting them the perfect table on the viewing deck at the resort brasserie. And the usual ones that happened every time he was near. Hyper-aware tingles tuned to his contours, and the way he moved…the shift of his muscular shoulders, that physical confidence he had.

He'd been easy to spot on the slopes because he was the best. Over and over again he'd come hurtling down, flying off jumps, looping and twisting, somersaulting. She'd felt his adrenaline pumping through her own veins, felt his raw energy burning inside her. He'd looked so wild and free, so powerful. Sexy as hell…like on the couch, in his faded red shirt, with his hair still damp from swimming. She felt a tug, desire stirring. She couldn't forget the taste of him, the way his lips had felt on hers, the way they'd melted into each other, all tenderness and heat, then hunger rising and rising, oh, and the warm bliss of his hands on her body, his fingers teasing, that sweet ache—

'Simone, how long before I can do the things Papa does?'

She blinked. Yann was looking at her with serious eyes. 'How long?' She had to hold in a smile. Yann had barely touched his lunch. He'd been pressed to the rail, watching Dax. She'd stolen a picture on her phone—a son in the act of hero-worshipping his father—and texted it to Dax, just in case he ever needed reassurance about where he stood with Yannick. She took a breath, letting her smile out. 'To be honest, I'm not sure, but starting young is good and now you've got your board, and the best teacher in the world, then I think you'll learn quickly.' She looked at Chloe. 'And you will too. You'll both come on fast with Dax teaching you.'

'*See.*' Chloe was giving Yann a look. 'We're *both* going to be good.'

Yann grinned, then they started bumping shoulders, messing about. They were hungry, getting to the silly stage of tired. She looked up, scanning for Dax. The market was busy, full of glow and the sweet smell of crepes cooking, full of energetic-looking types in vibrant gear. Like Dax. 'Vibrant' summed him up perfectly. He was atomic, energetic, completely gorgeous, and—

Her mouth dried. There he was, standing near a stall, talking to a girl, a stunning girl in a bright blue parka. He was smiling and nodding, rocking back on his heels a bit, and the girl was talking and laughing, touching him, little touches, then longer ones, more like holding really, her blue-gloved hands on his forearms, her fingers going round, holding, holding on…

Simone looked down, seeing spots, hearing the blood roaring in her ears. Dax had mentioned his free-rider friends before. Pals, buddies, male friends, but of course there had to have been 'girl friends' too, and *girlfriends*… poised elegant girls like Blue Parka Girl.

Of course.

She gulped a breath, searching her mouth for moisture. Last night, after Yann had almost caught them, she'd back-pedalled, scared of getting close to Dax, scared for herself and for Chloe… And Dax had back-pedalled too, for Yann. They'd agreed that what had happened between them shouldn't have. But in spite of that, all day long it had felt that there was something still going on between them, something warm and wonderful flowing back and forth every time their eyes had met, and even though they'd agreed that the kiss had been a mistake, that bright, lovely thing shuttling between them had felt golden, like something to treasure. But now it felt as if it was being ripped away by a girl in a blue parka and she couldn't stand it... couldn't bear it!

Oh, God!

She gripped the table, head swimming. Last night, she'd told herself she couldn't let herself get close to Dax because she'd always be anxious about his free riding, because if anything happened to him then everything would come crashing down...but what was this feeling if not a crashing-down feeling? She was crashing hard, melting down, jealous of Blue Parka Girl. Feeling sick, feeling wronged, feeling too many churning emotions to count. She swallowed hard. Which could only mean that it was too late. *Too late!* She already *cared* about Dax, more than cared. *Oh, God!* She was in deep!

She drew a ragged breath and looked up. He was kissing the girl's cheeks, saying goodbye, his smile wide, his eyes all twinkly. Did they have plans for later? Her heart twisted. *Stop!* She needed to compartmentalise. Distract herself. *Fast!*

She looked at the kids, forcing out a smile. 'I think your hot chocolate is coming.' She frisked her hands together. 'Won't that be nice? Something hot to drink! Are you guys cold? Because I'm cold, freezing—'

'Perfect timing, then!' Dax was at her shoulder, sliding a tray onto the bleached timber table. He slipped onto the bench beside her. 'Sorry that took a while. They ran out of *vin chaud*. I had to wait for them to make a new batch.'

Why couldn't she look at him? Why couldn't she stop her stomach from writhing? She passed serviettes to the kids, who were already tucking into their chocolate twists. 'It's fine. No need to apologise.' And then suddenly more words slid off some sharp edge on her tongue. 'It must have been *nice and warm* over by the stalls.'

There was a stinging silence, then the spots were flashing again, and regret was streaming through her veins. What was wrong with her? She was out of control. She had to rein it in. *Had to!* And then she felt his hand settling between her shoulder blades.

'If you're too cold we can go somewhere else.' There was a dry patch in his voice, a sort of crack, like thin ice breaking. 'We don't have to stay here…'

Her heart shrivelled. She'd hurt him. The last thing she ever wanted to do. She took a breath, trying to find a piece of steadiness. 'No, it's fine, really. I'm sorry.' She swallowed hard, forcing herself to look up. He looked bleached, his eyes loud and bruised. Her fault! But how to explain? How to make it right? She took a breath. 'I'm sorry. What I said came out all wrong…' *Breathe!* 'I'm not that cold.' She dug out a smile. 'How could I be in this lovely cosy jacket?' Something flickered behind his eyes. 'I just meant that it was probably warmer where you…' Her stomach tightened. 'But I'm fine.'

'Are you?' He tilted his head. 'Because we could go inside somewhere…' His gaze was searching, too hard to hold.

She looked at the kids, tucking in, all rosy-cheeked. They'd all had such a great day, because of Dax, because of his kindnesses. That was what she'd been thinking about before Blue Parka Girl had thrown her into a flat spin. That was what she needed to tell him, so he'd know how much he was appreciated.

She turned back to him. 'No, honestly. I want to stay here. It's lovely…the lights, and the nice smells, and the festive vibes! It was a good idea to come!' She felt warmth for him rising inside like light. 'You've given us such a fantastic day, Dax. I've loved every minute of it, the resort, Chamonix, seeing the streets and the horse traps. And now this!' The tension in his eyes was fading. She felt relief bubbling up, a smile spilling out. 'The cold might be freezing my cheeks off, but I don't want to be anywhere else.'

His gaze was clearing, warmth coming back in. 'Okay.' He picked up the *vin chaud* and put it into her hands, a smile touching his lips. 'Well, hopefully this will unfreeze your cheeks!'

'Thanks.' She slid her hands around it, nosing the warm cinnamon and clove aromas to hide the sudden wetness in her eyes. He was so lovely. No wonder she was feeling what she was feeling, but she couldn't do anything about it because he'd agreed with her, hadn't he, that their kiss had been a mistake? Yann was his priority, and, though he hadn't said it, he had his commitments to his sponsors too, the big 'adventure' he was planning. She shuddered around her glass. She'd just have to keep her feelings locked up: the deep ones, the jealous ones. She absolutely couldn't sting him like that again. He didn't deserve it. And *she* needed to remember why she was here: for Chloe, for Yann, and there was the money too.

She felt a sudden nudge, Dax's shoulder bumping hers. 'By the way, I got you this too.' A delicious-looking piece of flan slid into view. 'They said it was a special Christmas recipe...'

Yann was bouncing up and down on his bottom. 'I can't wait to try my board tomorrow!'

Full of life! Was this the same boy he'd brought back to Paris a few months ago? It didn't seem like it. This bouncy version of Yannick reminded him of himself. He pinned the duvet over Yann's knees, restraining him gently. 'Tomorrow will be here before you know it, especially if you settle down and go to sleep. Snowboarders need their rest so they're sharp on the slopes, so they don't make mistakes.'

'I was watching you the whole time today.' Yann collapsed backwards into his pillow. 'You didn't make any mistakes.'

He smiled. Just as well Yann's eyes weren't attuned to nuances yet. Being out there again had been a blast, but a few times he hadn't sailed high enough to pull off the somersaults as seamlessly as he'd wanted, and some of his landings had been a little off, but he'd been away for a while, hadn't he? So no surprise! A few more resort sessions would oil his wheels, and then he'd be good for the wild stuff. For now, he could use Yann's misapprehension to his advantage.

He shifted, tucking the duvet around Yann's chest. 'That's because I had a good night's sleep.' *White lie!* He'd actually had a restless night, thinking about Simone and the kiss and about her losing André so close to Christmas— December the seventeenth—how that must have felt, and then he'd been thinking about Yann's unexpected interest in snowboarding, feeling stoked about it. Maybe lack of sleep, and the little entourage—*his son*—watching from the restaurant deck had affected his performance on the slopes too. He'd only ever ridden for himself before—for satisfaction, for personal validation, for sponsorship money—but today he'd felt a sudden overwhelming desire to impress Yann, so that Yann would look up to him, admire him, see him as a father to be proud of. He'd never had that…a father to look up to, a father to share things with. It was the hole in his soul he'd learned to ignore, but on the slopes it had come to him that Yann's interest in snowboarding was a line he could ride, a line that might, one day, take him all the way into Yann's heart.

He finished with the duvet and sat back. It was already doing something, changing things. Yann was looking at him openly now, his eyes full of light and mystery. He felt a little pang in his chest. Zara had used to look at him like this. Could this be a Zara moment…? Could he make it into one somehow? His stomach tightened. Saying the wrong thing could mess things up, but Simone had said he should try and who'd have known better than her? She'd been there, got the tee shirt. He swallowed hard. He wasn't exactly comfortable, but this wasn't about *him*. He needed to try, for Yannick.

He took a breath and reached a slow hand to Yann's head, touching the springy dark hair that felt exactly like his own. Yann blinked but he didn't pull away. That was good. Encouraging! He licked his lips. 'Your eyes are just like your *maman*'s, you know.'

A shadow flitted across Yann's face.

His chest panged. Flitting shadows weren't good. He gulped a breath, clutching at straws. 'But I guess you know that already… I mean, people must say it…must have said it before.'

Lame!

Yann let out a little sigh.

His mouth turned to dust. Now what? He was looking at a stop sign. He swallowed hard, twirling one of Yann's curls around his finger and then suddenly he noticed Yann's eyes flickering, drooping a little. His breath caught. Had Zara played with Yann's hair like this? And then a memory surfaced. Hot nights, tangled sheets, lying in Zara's arms, her hands in his own hair, playing, twirling, always twirling.

Of course!

He felt a warm tide rising, a sudden peacefulness. 'Your *maman* liked your hair, didn't she?'

Yann nodded, his eyes drooping a little more.

He twirled his fingers for a while, then flattened his hand, stroking his son's dark curls, watching him drifting, feeling a strange tightness in his chest, an urge he couldn't contain. He leaned over, pressing his lips to Yann's forehead. 'She liked mine too.'

For a heartbeat Yann's hand connected with the place above his ear, and then he was turning, settling for sleep.

He felt a lump thickening in his throat. Had Yann's warm little touch been meant for him, or had it been a sleepy reflex meant for Zara? He breathed in slowly, deeply, feeling the weight of his mistakes pressing down on him all over again. He should have been better with Yann from the start. He'd filled Yann's room with toys, just as Colette had done with him, and then he'd given up when Yann hadn't fallen over himself with gratitude and joy. If it weren't for Simone's advice, he'd still have been getting it wrong, missing out on this strange, wonderful thing that was happening.

If it weren't for Simone...

He got to his feet, watching Yann for a moment longer, then he slipped out of the room and padded downstairs. In the hall he stood, listening to the low sound of the television coming from the den. Simone was in there, waiting for him, but he couldn't go in, not yet. He needed to be alone, needed space to think.

He went to his office and fell into the easy chair. That edge on Simone's voice at the Christmas market and the desperate apologies that followed were niggling him. They'd moved past it, smoothed it so flat that he couldn't bring himself to ask her about it now, but still, it was bothering him. He wasn't good at leaving things alone: dripping taps, leaky boots, loaded tones.

He sighed. He just didn't get it. They'd had such a great day. Perfect weather! Buzzing resort! He'd got them a good table for lunch and, after his last run of the day, he'd taken them around Cham, pointing out the cool places. Simone had been sparkling, teasing him in the ski shop, smiling down at her new boots. In spite of the kissing mistake, it had felt as if something bright and alive was still flowing between them and he'd liked it. *Loved it!*

But then something changed. One minute she'd been all smiles, forcing money on him for the drinks, and the next, she'd been tight-lipped and spiky. A different person. It had knocked the wind out of him, killed his buzz. He'd felt flattened. *Hurt!*

He swallowed hard. It had pitched him backwards to his childhood. Colette, one minute warm and smiling, 'dying' to see the picture he was drawing for her, the next too busy with some waste-of-space loser to even look up from her champagne flute. And those soirées…taking his hand, leading him around like an exhibit, until some fawning sycophant had caught her interest. He'd been forgotten in the pop of a champagne cork. The next day, she'd be all over him again, playing the devoted mother, taking him to some fancy shop to buy him something he didn't want. With Colette, he'd never known which way the cards were going to fall. At fourteen, he'd seized the pack and dealt himself the cards he wanted. Money? Yes! School? No! Skateboarding? Yes! All day, every day! And at sixteen, he'd left, taking the credit card she'd given him when he was fifteen so he could 'sort himself out' with food or whatever during her frequent long weekends away. She'd always paid it off, no matter how much he ran up, because she was generous like that!

He got to his feet, pacing. Holding all the cards, calling all the shots was the only way not to get hurt, the only way he could be sure of not hurting anyone else. Honesty was key. With women, he always told them the truth upfront, made sure they knew he was only interested in physical kicks. No strings, no tomorrows, no heartbreak. But with Simone, he'd had to start in a different place. And he'd felt safe in her hands because she'd been kind and honest and wise, and yet still, even Simone, the only woman he'd ever trusted, had changed in a heartbeat, exactly like Colette!

He raked a hand through his hair. Except she wasn't like Colette, not at all! There had to have been a reason for the snarky tone she'd used on him, something he was missing. *Think!* She'd been fine when he'd gone off for the drinks, cool and stiff when he'd got back. There was something in between he wasn't seeing.

'*It must have been nice and warm over by the stalls...*'

Nice and warm...

Nice and warm...

His pulse jumped.

Pascale!

Had Simone seen him with Pascale? But why would that have upset her? Unless... Unless maybe she'd thought that he was *into* Pascale? But how on earth...? Was it Pascale being all over him? He blinked. But that was just Pascale. Touchy-feely! Just a touchy-feely friend, whereas Simone...

What was Simone?

He felt warmth swelling in his chest. Simone was more than a friend. Much more... She could turn him inside out with just a look, could stop his heart with a smile. Didn't she know that? Hadn't she felt it in his kiss? Or did she think, because he'd agreed it was a mistake, that it hadn't meant anything?

He felt a frown coming, confusion tangling inside. She'd said she'd kissed him because she was lonely, because it was a bad time of year. He'd got the impression that maybe, in her head, she'd been kissing André. It had stung, but if he was on the right beat about Pascale, if Simone had felt jealous of Pascale, then… His pulse quickened. Then maybe everything he'd felt in her kiss had been real after all—real for *him*, Dax, not André—the way she'd melted into him with soft little sighs, the way it had all felt so perfect…

He sat down again, heart pumping. But what to do? How to even make sense of all the things he was feeling about Simone? Like the way he loved talking to her and hearing her thoughts, even when they challenged his own. Like the way he loved spoiling her and Chloe just to see them smiling, just to feel their warmth flowing back. Like wanting Simone to believe in him, and in his sport, and in his sense for the mountain, so that she wouldn't be worried. Like wanting her to be proud of the way he was learning to be a parent.

He squeezed his eyes shut. He didn't just like Simone, he was crazy about her, but he couldn't march into the den and pull her into his arms, no matter how much he wanted to. They'd been there once and stepped back. Picking it up again would be a conscious decision, a commitment, and what did he know about commitment? It was what Simone would want, was no less than she deserved, but he didn't do love, didn't do relationships! He'd learned at his mother's knee that being close to someone only led to pain. He didn't want to feel pain or inflict it on anyone else, especially not Simone. The thought of hurting her the way he'd been hurt by Colette scared him more than riding down the steepest cliff.

He rubbed the back of his neck. And this wasn't just about him. Yann was coming out of his shell, letting him in, giving him something back...that little touch as he'd turned to go to sleep! Yann was happy, having a good time with Chloe, and with Simone, and with *him*! He couldn't risk changing the dynamic, risk embarking on something that could go wrong, that could chase away the only two people who mattered to his son.

He drew in a breath and stood up. He'd have to content himself with caring for Simone as a friend. He could still laugh with her, still talk to her, and enjoy her company. Being friends was safe. He could live with that. It was a win-win, for everybody.

CHAPTER NINE

December 17th

'MUSH! MUSH! MUSH!' Chloe was calling out to the dogs, flicking her arms for good measure.

Simone laughed all the way from her belly. Chloe was having the best time ever, and so was she, swooping through a frosted landscape behind a team of huskies. It was just like the picture on the dog-sledding website, except this was real. Completely perfect! High blue sky, sun catching at her eyes, Chloe in front, giggling. The pace was gentle, but the breeze on her face and the sound of the runners sloughing through the snow was making it feel faster somehow.

She twisted her head to look back at Dax, felt her heart filling. He'd planned this outing specially, to help her get through the anniversary of André's death. He hadn't said it, but she knew. It had been there in his eyes. It was classic Dax. Kind! Thoughtful!

His sunglasses glinted, then he was smiling, his voice coming over the swishing snow. 'Are you all right?'

Her heart filled again. He was always looking at her with that melting gaze he had, asking her if she was all right, making her feel cared for. *Cherished!* It made her want to throw her arms around him and tell him that he was cherished too. It made her want to tell him all the things she was holding inside, all the deep wonderful feelings that were growing and growing. She was a dam ready to burst. That was what it felt like.

She pushed up her sunglasses wanting him to see everything she was feeling. 'I'm better than all right! It's the best thing ever!'

He laughed, circling his hand. 'Eyes forward! You've got dogs to drive.'

She turned back, chuckling. *Dogs to drive!* The dogs seemed to know where they were going without any help from her. They were capering along panting misty breaths, tails going. It was all so lovely, dashing through the snowy pines with steep peaks rising through the mist in the distance. It was a sad day, yes, but she couldn't make herself feel sad because Chloe was in front trilling a happy little song from her favourite movie, and Dax was there, right behind her, filling her well.

She felt warmth pulsing through her veins.

Dax was always filling her well, such as when he'd miraculously 'dug out' an old snowboard for her, a board that looked suspiciously brand new, so she could join in with Chloe and Yann's basic snowboard training. He'd held her waist from behind, gliding his board along with hers, keeping her straight, steadying her when she wobbled. It had felt wonderful, the board moving, his hands right there, his body behind hers, their breaths billowing and tingling, a special moment that had felt intimate even though Chloe and Yann had been watching.

That was Dax! Always giving. Even though he'd been busy on the slopes—the safe resort slopes, thank goodness—getting himself back to mountain fitness, busy with testing and reviewing kit for his sponsors and padding his social media feeds, he'd somehow still found time to organise some private ice-skating lessons for the kids, and he'd set them up with a block of skiing lessons too. All that, and what had she done? Stung him with her jealous words at the Christmas market, and even though it had happened days ago, and even though it hadn't put a dent in things, it was still a stone in her shoe, a constant irritation that she wanted to shake out.

She wanted to explain herself, open up her heart, but every time she'd tried the words had dried on her tongue, because explaining would have meant unravelling everything, going back to the kiss that they'd agreed was a mistake, and it had made her think about how she'd felt that night when Yann had come downstairs, how close a shave it had been, how it could have spoiled everything for Dax and his son. And then she'd thought about Chloe, about what they could both lose if she got tangled up with Dax and something happened to him. And when she'd thought of all that, it had seemed too big to talk about, too heavy, so she'd held it in.

But now Dax had done it again, surprised her with dog sledding, to take her mind off André. And he'd succeeded, except that it wasn't the dog sledding that was taking her mind off André. It was *him*! Everything he was. Handsome. Kind. Thoughtful. Generous. Her heart was full to the brim and there wasn't a thing she could do about it. She was deep in, falling deeper… What to do? How long could she keep these feelings in? She dropped her sunglasses over her eyes, gripping the sled handle hard. Not much longer. She didn't want to. No matter how complicated things were, she wanted to take that risk, tell him how she felt, shout it from the top of Mont Blanc. She was falling for Dax D'Aureval!

'That was so great!' Simone was all smiles. Beautiful. Radiant! Eyes, cheeks, lips. Perfect in her red jacket and the green hat he'd given her in Paris. She was perfect full stop.

He grinned. 'You're a natural musher.'

'Hmm…' She widened her eyes at him. 'Not so much at the beginning…'

The sight of her jogging—slipping and sliding—alongside the sled as the dogs fell into their running rhythm, then trying to jump on, had tickled him and Yann to bits. He felt his grin widening, sliding into goofiness. 'The getting-on part is always tricky…'

'It wasn't for you!' Her eyebrows slid up. 'You just leapt on.'

'I think we got the geriatric dogs, so—you know—slower.' He shot a glance at the kids, who were busy making a fuss of the huskies. 'They were too slow for Yann anyway.'

She chuckled. 'Actual light is too slow for Yann! He's high octane, like you!' Her hands went to the beanie, making some tiny invisible adjustment, then they fell again. 'Anyway, it was a lovely surprise. Thank you.' Her gaze tightened on his, something flickering behind it. 'You're very thoughtful, Dax.'

He drew in a careful breath. So she knew, or had guessed, that he'd organised the dog sledding to lighten her day! *This* day, the seventeenth… If she could read him that easily, what else was she reading on his face? Could she see how much he wanted to kiss her?

Her gaze softened, radiating warmth. 'Just so you know, I'm really okay about it being the day it is.' She took a little breath, a smile ghosting on her lips. 'I'm happy, you know, just being here. With you…' He felt his pulse quickening. Was she trying to tell him something, or was that just his own wishful thinking—?

'Yoh, Dax!'

She startled and he did too, but the voice ringing across the compound was familiar and dear. He threw his hand up. 'Hey, Victor!' He shot Simone a quick look. 'Victor's a buddy. He owns this place.'

'Ahh!' She took a backwards step. 'I'll leave you to catch up, then.' She smiled, dazzling him, then she grimaced, cartoon-style. 'Chloe's wanted a dog for ever, so I'd better go check she isn't stuffing a husky under her jacket!' She turned, walking away, her hair flowing from under the beanie, catching the breeze, glinting in the sun.

He felt a tug. Caring about Simone as a friend had been a good plan…in theory. The problem was, he couldn't seem to shoehorn his feelings into the friendship mould. He'd tried. He'd got her a snowboard so she could join in with Yann and Chloe's lessons but then hadn't been able to resist helping her balance by riding his board behind her with his hands on her waist, just to be near her, just to touch her. She was in his head all the time, messing with his pulse, making his chest go tight, then fuzzy, and the more time he spent with her, the worse it was getting. And maybe she was feeling it too because just now it had felt as if she was trying to tell him something significant. Victor's timing sucked!

'Hey, man!' Victor was stepping up, beaming.

'Hey, Vic! How's it going?' He held out his hand. 'I thought you'd be out skiing.'

Victor pumped his hand, then landed a few hearty slaps on his back. 'No. I'm playing midwife today.' He chuckled. 'We're having puppies!'

'Nice!'

'It's so good to see you, Dax! It's been a while, huh?' His eyes narrowed. 'What are you doing here? Don't tell me you're sledding?'

'Yep! We just got back!' He took a breath. 'Family outing.'

Victor's mouth fell ajar. '*Family* outing?'

He felt his cheeks growing warm. Victor wasn't in the loop. Very few of his buddies were. He nodded. 'That's right. I have a son.' He motioned to the kids. 'He's over there with his friend. His name is Yannick.'

Victor turned to look. 'Christ! Mini-Dax! How did—?'

He cut in. 'It's a long story.' One he didn't want to get into at that moment. 'I'll tell you another time.'

'Okay.' Victor's eyes gleamed. 'And who's the lovely lady? Yann's *maman*?'

'No. Simone's my…' He looked over. She was bending to pet the dogs, laughing at something the kids were saying. He swallowed. 'She looks after Yannick when I'm riding. The little girl is her daughter, Chloe, Yann's best friend.'

Victor swung round to look, then swung back, scratching his ear. 'I'm impressed! You've got yourself quite a little family there.'

For some reason, he didn't feel the slightest inclination to protest.

He grinned. 'You're not doing too badly yourself! Puppies, huh?'

'Funny!' Victor rolled his eyes. 'I'm planning ahead! Some of the dogs will be retiring soon. This is our second litter this winter.' He shifted on his feet. 'Hey! If you're not in a dash, maybe Yann and Chloe would like to come and play with older puppies for a while. They need socialising.' He let out a hearty chuckle. 'The puppies, I mean, not the kids.'

His heart pulsed. With the kids out of the way, maybe he and Simone could pick up their conversation. 'They'd love it, I'm sure!' He threw an arm around Victor's shoulders and started walking him towards the kids. 'Chloe's desperate for a dog, apparently, so cuddling some puppies is going to be right up her street!'

'It's like a fairy tale!' Simone was turning slowly, looking up and around, her voice hushed and full of wonder. 'There aren't even any footprints. It's like no one's ever been here before!'

She was right. The glade was pristine, shimmering with lemony light, plushily silent.

'Maybe they haven't. Victor only completed it last year.' He felt his stomach churning. So much for picking up their earlier conversation! They were out of sight of the compound now, starting along the woodland trail, a perfect, private spot, and suddenly he was tongue-tied, full of doubts, reduced to making polite conversation. *I'm happy...just being here. With you...'* It had sounded as if she was trying to tell him something, but what if he was wrong? If he blew it, it would spoil the happy day he'd planned.

She was coming round to face him again, an irresistible bundle of red jacket, and green beanie, and glossy hair, and those eyes, holding his, turning him inside out, tying his knots into knots.

He swallowed a dry edge in his mouth. 'He wants to pull in summer visitors. So there's a woodland walk. Picnic areas. He's talking about putting in an adventure playground for the kids.'

'Anything that keeps kids entertained is a bonus.' A smile touched her lips. 'Like puppies…'

Even that sounded like an oblique message. Or was he just losing the plot altogether?

She tilted her head slightly. 'So…have you known Victor a long time?'

He bit his teeth together. 'Yeah. Vic's a free skier. We used to—' He clamped his mouth shut. He couldn't do this, small-talking. He didn't know whether he was coming or going, imagining signs or not, but it was time to seize the pack, start dealing the cards he wanted. He closed the distance between them, fastening his eyes on hers. 'Look, Simone, I don't want to talk about Victor.' He could feel his pulse pounding through his skin. 'I want to talk about us.'

She blinked. 'Us?'

'Yes…' His pulse was in his ears now, hammering softly. 'You said back there that you were happy here, *with me*, and the way you said it…well…it felt like you were trying to tell me something, but I don't know…' he swallowed, trying to read the changing landscape in her eyes '…and I want to…need to.'

Her mouth was working, and then her eyes filled, gleaming, tugging his heart right out. 'What if I *was* trying to tell you something?'

She took a breath. 'What if I was trying to tell you that you make me happy all the time, every day? What if...?' Her eyes were reaching in, taking him apart. 'What if I were to tell you that, that... I care about you, Dax?' He felt his ribs loosening, tenderness rushing in. 'And what if I just didn't know how to say it because I wasn't sure?' Her lips stiffened. 'Because we said it was a mistake...'

His heart pulsed. 'Oh, Simone...' He felt a powerful warmth rising inside, a slew of emotions he couldn't name. 'Maybe it just felt like a mistake at the time because of Yann.' He put his hands on her shoulders, tightening his gaze on hers, loading it with everything he was feeling. 'But now, all I know is that whatever we started, I can't seem to switch it off. I can't make myself not want to be with you.'

The gleam in her eyes turned to a bright warm glow. 'And I can't make myself not want to be with you either.'

For a beat, his breath stopped and then he couldn't hold back. He took her face in his hands and lowered his mouth to hers, wanting to show her all the things he was feeling inside, things he couldn't even name. Her lips were perfect, meltingly warm, yielding, and suddenly he was burning up inside, exploding, his senses skewing just as they had the first time. He pulled her in hard, deep kissing, losing himself in the heat of her mouth, the maddeningly sweet taste of her, until she was moaning softly, pulling him in, tangling her fingers in his hair and it was too much but not enough. He hooked his arm around her waist, lowering her into the snow, kissing her face, her neck, her mouth again, feeling his veins blazing, feeling her body moving, rising against him, and then she was holding his face, stroking his cheeks, burning his lips with hers until his breath was broken.

He pulled away, pulse racing, taking in the flush in her cheeks, the haze in her eyes. Her lips looked red and full. His felt scorched. He wanted her with every fibre of his being, but not here, in the snow, with the clock running down. When he made love to her, he wanted to do it slowly, and in comfort. He drew in a breath, combing a lock of hair away from her cheek with his finger, looking into the soft glow of her gaze. 'Are you all right?'

'More than all right.' She smiled a slow smile. 'You're always asking me that.'

'Because I always want to know.' He kissed her, feeling a fresh tug of desire. 'And since I seem to have thrown you to the ground, I definitely need to know because I might have to check for injuries!'

She started to giggle. 'No injuries!' She put

her hand to his face. 'And you didn't throw me down. I think I was going dizzy, and you caught me!'

'Dizzy doesn't sound good.' Her touch and the look in her eyes were messing with his pulse, making his own head swim.

'It was fine!' Her lips curved up. 'It was the *best* kind of dizzy.'

'Ah, that kind!' She was irresistible, almost too lovely to look at. 'I think I'm feeling it right now, looking at you.'

'And you looking is making me feel it again.' He kissed her nose, then shifted, propping himself up on his elbow. 'We should just stay like this for a while until it passes.'

'It won't pass.' She turned her head, trapping him in a soft twinkly gaze. 'That's the problem I have with you, Dax D'Aureval. You make me dizzy all the time.'

'Right back at you.' He felt his throat thickening, something welling up inside. He swallowed. 'From that very first moment.'

'At the bistro door...' Her eyes filled with a gleam. 'Me too.'

Snowflakes melting on her eyelashes, that luminous smile. He traced a finger over her cheek, feeling its coolness, its softness, feeling a rush of tenderness. 'My first thought was: Snow Angel.'

Her eyes filled. 'That's so…romantic.' And then her lips quirked and suddenly she was giggling. 'You were Monsieur Blue Jacket, which isn't very imaginative, but I was, you know, dizzy!'

'You were perfect.'

She pulled a screwy face. 'Erm, no! My hair was a mess, and I had panda eyes.'

'I didn't notice. I just saw you.'

Her eyes held him for a beat, and then she chuckled. 'God, you're a smooth talker! Do you practise in the mirror?'

He grinned. 'Every day.'

She smiled, and then she was wriggling away from him. 'We should make a move. The kids will be wondering where we are.'

'They're knee-deep in puppies. They don't care where we are.'

'Come on!' She was sitting up, tugging at his sleeve. 'We should get back.'

He jumped up, pulling her to her feet, then he picked up the beanie.

'I'll have to say I fell.' She was looking down at her jeans, rubbing at the damp patches.

'Well, it's the truth! Kind of!'

'Funny!' She flicked him a smile that made his heart skip.

Snow Angel! God, she was lovely, and she cared about him, in spite of her misgivings about his free riding. *That* was really something! His stomach tightened. Could he be as strong for her, not cause her any pain? Was he going to be any good at the relationship thing? It was all so new, and it wasn't as if they only had themselves to think about. Was being a little bit scared acceptable?

She was smoothing her hair now, scanning the ground for the beanie.

'I've got it!'

She looked up. 'Ah!'

He brushed it off, then stepped in, fitting it to her head, feeling her eyes warming his face. He met her gaze. Scared or not, he couldn't not want her, couldn't not want to try being everything she needed. He put a hand to her cheek. 'Sim, just so we're absolutely clear, this isn't a mistake, okay?'

'I know.' She smiled, and then her eyes became serious. 'But we should talk about the practicalities.'

'You mean the kids?'

She nodded. 'We need to be discreet.'

'In case it turns out to be a mistake?'

She nodded, frowning a bit. 'Not very romantic, is it? But I suppose that's the way it is with kids...' She gave a little shrug. 'I haven't exactly been here before.'

'Me neither, but you already know that.' It

wasn't romantic, but squaring things away was good. They had to protect the kids. 'I agree about being discreet.' He took a breath. 'Also, I need to tell you something…'

A shadow crossed her face. 'What?'

His chest panged. She was such a worrier. He tugged her close, looking into her eyes. 'It's nothing bad, just something you should know.' He could feel his heart drumming, a prickling at the back of his neck. Was it ridiculous to be feeling embarrassed? He took a deep breath. 'I'm a relationship virgin.'

Her face stretched. 'Really? You've never…' And then her expression softened. 'I suppose all the travelling's not exactly conducive…'

'No. No, it isn't.' He felt a prick of guilt. It was only a white lie and it could well have been true! Travelling *was* a barrier to relationships unless your girlfriend was into the free-riding scene. The truth could wait. He didn't want to be unravelling his inner psyche right now, getting into all his Colette hang-ups. Simone was in his arms in a snowy glade with lemony light catching her eyes. All too soon they'd be back with the kids. Right now, all he wanted to do was kiss her.

CHAPTER TEN

Later...

'DO YOU KNOW what I feel like?' Dax was twinkling at the kids, making their eyes dance. 'I feel like making fondue! Who'd like to help?'

Chloe and Yann both yelled, 'Me!' then burst out laughing.

Dax laughed too and then his eyes found hers, full of slow burn and the secret they were keeping.

She felt her breath catch, her insides turning to liquid. She could hardly believe what had happened between them in the woods, could hardly believe that they were starting something after all, taking a chance on each other. She felt a smile coming, a rush of pure joy behind it. 'Are two helpers enough or do you need me too?'

'You can spectate for now.' He grinned, flashing his eyebrows in that mischievous way he had. 'You're probably still catching your breath, huh?'

She felt a giggle vibrating in her belly. He was speaking in riddles for the kids' sake, but she could read him. He wasn't only alluding to their tumble in the snow and all the kisses they'd shared on the way back to the sledding centre. He was teasing her about the luge, the luge on rails alpine coaster that had been his second surprise of the day.

After they'd peeled the kids off the puppies, he'd driven them to Domaine des Planards amusement park. 'The luge is good fun,' he'd said. 'It's not as fast as the real thing, but I think you'll handle it.'

'Me?' She'd felt her stomach collapsing. She hated roller coasters, hated the feeling of not being in control, and the toboggans that were flying along the rails and screaming around the tight bends had looked insanely quick. Not her thing at all. She'd tried to put her foot down. 'I'm not going on that!'

'Simone!' He'd leaned in, squeezing her elbow, breathing words into her ear. 'I'm bigging it up for Yann and Chloe! Kids three years and over can ride this thing, but they have to be accompanied by an adult, which means you've got to ride it.' Big, brown eyes—not so innocent eyes—had fastened on hers. 'You *can* control the speed if you want to, but where's the fun in that?' His eyebrows had flickered out a challenge. 'Brakes are for wimps!'

She held in a smile. The tow up had seemed interminable. She'd plastered on her game face for Chloe's sake, fake smiling and waving at Dax when he'd turned around from the toboggan in front to throw her a cheeky grin. Chloe had been in the front seat, chattering away nonchalantly about the puppies, her little feet twitching against the footrests. Simone had made the appropriate responses, but the serene blue sky and the steady green pines ahead, and the skiers blithely whizzing past on the slopes around them, had seemed like a cruel taunt, a happy world away from the gnawing in her belly and from the rhythmic, metallic clunk of the toboggan as it went up, and up, and up. And then there'd been that jolting halt at the top, watching Dax and Yann's toboggan taking off, disappearing round the first bend at full pelt.

They'd had to wait another interminable minute before their own toboggan had started its death dive. Instantly, Chloe had let out an excited little screech, following it with whoops and deep, rolling chuckles. Simone's stomach had been dipping and clenching, performing acrobatics, but then somehow all that had seemed to stop, and the speed had started to feel exhilarating. Suddenly, she'd been laughing too, leaning into the experience, soaking it up, going with it instead of fighting it. By the third bend, she'd abandoned the brake, had heard her own squeals soaring with Chloe's, flying free on the wind as the speed and the G-force had tugged and pulled, and it had felt terrifying and thrilling and empowering all at the same time.

When she'd tumbled off with Chloe at the end of the ride, high as kite and tingling all over, Dax had been waiting, his eyes merry and wicked. 'So, are you up for another go?'

She gave herself a little hug inside. She'd jumped at the chance! *Her!* Simone scaredy-cat Cossart! They'd ended up having three more goes, swapping round so they each got two rides with Yann and two with Chloe. Afterwards, Dax had taken them for crepes. And now, he was showing Chloe and Yann how to rub cut garlic around the fondue pot, looking every perfect inch of him like the perfect father.

'It adds a nice flavour.' His eyes lifted to hers, flickering. 'Makes the fondue even more tasty.'

Her pulse spiked. Dax could turn her inside out with a single glance. She felt a rush of happiness, a mad tingling in her belly. Everything was opening up between them, unfolding, and it felt so good. Yes, things were complicated, but the direction of travel felt right. Going forwards. Going forwards at last, after three long years of simply existing.

She looked at Chloe. She was looking up at Dax with shining eyes. André's eyes! Chloe was so like André. Her smile, her frown, just like his. She felt a tug of sadness, strangely, not for herself, but for André's parents. In spite of what day it was, she was on top of the world, but they had nothing, only photographs and emptiness. She felt a lump thickening in her throat. They could have had so much more. They could have been seeing what she was seeing now: André living on in his daughter. They'd cut off their noses to spite their faces. So sad. So stupid! How could they have let their grief shut them in like that, cutting them off from love and happiness, and all the things in life that were still good, and pure, and true? All the things she was feeling for Dax.

Dax! Supervising Yann with pouring beer into the fondue pot, and at the same time directing Chloe to a shelf in the fridge to get the cheese, smiling the whole time. He was something else!

She slipped off her stool and leaned over the island unit. 'So, where did you learn to make fondue?'

He looked up briefly, and then he was setting the pot on the hob, lighting the gas, adjusting the flame until it was a small glow. 'Colette used to make it for me sometimes when I was little...' A shadow smudged his face. 'She used to let me help. My job was adding the Gruyère.' He turned to Chloe and Yann. 'Which is what you two are going to be doing in a minute. But first, we need to chop the cheese up. Chloe! How are your knife skills?'

Chloe's eyes popped. 'What are knife skills?'

'I guess that answers my question.' His eyes caught hers, his gaze steely. 'Simone, are you okay with me teaching Chloe some knife skills?'

Her breath stopped. Was he mad? The knife in his hand was hefty, glinting with sharp intent.

She shook her head. 'No! Definitely not. She's six!'

He shrugged, frowning. 'Don't you think it's good to teach kids this stuff when they're young? It's like snowboarding or playing the piano.'

She felt her neck prickling. 'No! Actually... no! Playing the piano is rather different from playing around with sharp objects—'

'Simone!' His lips were twitching, and then he was cracking up, laughing into her eyes. 'I was joking!' He was shaking his head at her, warm light twinkling in his eyes. 'You're *so* serious sometimes.'

He was right, she *was* serious, especially where Chloe was concerned. When it came to

Chloe, her protective radar was set to max. How could she even have thought he was being serious? He colour-coded his storage boxes, for pity's sake, kept his ropes and snowboards in impeccable rows. He wasn't reckless!

She shook her head. 'You got me!'

'Got you good!' He flashed a smile and then something openly seductive slipped into his gaze. 'So, I'm chopping the cheese; Chloe and Yann are going to throw it in; but we're going to need a responsible adult to do the stirring while I get on with cubing the bread.'

Responsible adult? He was up to something, luring her over. She held onto a smile, tingling inside. Being close to Dax was exactly where she wanted to be, near enough to catch the deep, warm scent of him. She moved around the island unit, watching him chopping and divvying up the cheese between the kids, until she was there at his side near the hob, standing close, feeling little sparks flying between them.

'Here.' He put a wooden spoon into her hands, his gaze steady except for a pinprick glow of mischief. 'Do you know the correct stirring action required for a fondue?'

She felt a smile aching in her cheeks. She was getting his drift, feeling a thrill of wickedness quivering in her belly. She held his gaze. 'To be honest, no, I'm not completely sure. I don't make fondue myself.'

His eyebrows flickered. 'In that case, I'll have to show you.' He moved in close. She breathed in the warm base notes of his cologne, felt the floor sliding under her feet. His eyes darkened. 'So you need to face the hob, obviously.'

She bit her lips together hard, holding onto the bubble of laughter that wanted to come out. 'Okay.' She sucked in a breath and turned her back to him. 'And I guess I put the spoon into the pot now…?'

One warm hand landed on her waist, followed a nanosecond later by the warm, gentle pressure of his whole body against her back. His voice was low. 'That's right.' His voice turned upbeat. 'Okay, kids, you can start adding the cheese… Yann! Not too much at once. Simone needs to stir it in…' His voice dropped again. 'She needs to melt it, slowly.' She felt the pressure of his body against hers increasing, felt a small gasp lodging in her throat. She looked at Chloe and Yann quickly. Their faces were fused in concentration over their separate bowls of cheese. She stirred slowly, pushing herself back, by degrees, against Dax, fighting a near impossible urge not to laugh out loud.

'Here…' His voice seemed to catch, and then it was trickling into her ear on a warm breath.

'I don't think you've got that quite right yet.' His right arm moved around hers, and then his hand was covering hers on the spoon, guiding her. 'Like this, see, round and round, so that all the cheese melts…slowly.'

'I think it's ready!' Yann was leaning over the pot, staring into it. 'I'm starving. I want to have some right now!'

'Me too.' Chloe looked up, and then her head tilted in a frown. 'Dax, did you do the bread yet?'

From behind, Dax produced a hearty cough that was full of unexploded laughter.

She stifled an explosion of her own, turning off the gas, and then she looked at Chloe. 'No, he hasn't. He's been slacking but I'm sure he's about to jump right to it.'

Dax sipped his beer, staring at the computer screen. Going over the route for his first proper free ride wasn't distracting him after all. He was still thinking about Simone, wondering why she'd disappeared into her room after they'd put the kids to bed. He tapped his teeth together. Was she all right? Had he done something wrong? He moused over the satellite picture of the couloir, zooming, and scrolling, feeling his stomach churning. She wasn't having second thoughts, surely…? *No!* She'd been warm and smiling all afternoon and through dinner,

sending him looks that had stopped his heart.
He sighed. Maybe the whole André anniversary thing was weighing on her, making her
feel awkward about the evening ahead, about
being alone with him. *Oh, God!* Did she think
he had expectations?

He set his beer down, heart going. He wanted
her, yes, more than anything, wanted to unwrap
her, very slowly, but it didn't have to be tonight.
If it was feeling wrong to her because it was the
anniversary of André's death, then he totally respected that! He could give her space, time, anything she wanted. He just wanted to know that
she was all right. Knowing for sure. That was
his thing. His insecurity. Courtesy of Colette!

He pushed the thought away, and moved the
mouse, tilting the image so he could see the
view from the summit. So different from the
side-on views. From the top, features flattened,
disappearing altogether sometimes. It was a
question of looking from all angles, holding the
shape of the line in your head. In spite of his jitters, he felt a smile coming. Simone's shape was
burned on his brain and he'd got a good idea of
her lines when she'd pushed back against him
stirring that fondue. Making fondue was relationship stuff! Having fun in the kitchen. Being
naughty! It had felt as hot as…but then Chloe

had called him out over the bread, and that had been that. *Family stuff!*

'Hey…'

Simone! He spun his chair and felt warmth taking him over. She was coming towards him, gorgeous in a low-necked blouse and dark jeans, her hair loose and gleaming. So *that* was what she'd been doing, trying to perfect perfection.

He got up, stepping out from the desk. 'Hey!'

She walked into his arms and lifted her face, smiling. 'I thought you might be in here.'

He kissed her, lingering for a moment, losing himself in the warmth of her lips, feeling the first hot lick of desire, and then he broke off. He was going to give her space, let *her* lead the way. He smiled. 'I was just checking something out.' He released her, stepping back. 'You look lovely.'

She tossed her hair then shot him a quirky little smile. 'Well, it's our first official date! I thought I should make an effort.' And then her eyes slid past him, narrowing. 'Meanwhile, you're playing computer games!'

He felt a smile creasing his cheeks. 'Not exactly, but I'll switch it off now.'

'No, don't.' She was going over to the desk. 'I'd like to see what you're looking at. It looks…weird.'

He followed her, catching the delicate scent

of her perfume. 'It's mountain porn, only interesting to mountaineers, but if you really want to see it…'

'I do.' She sat down and peered at the screen, her brow furrowing. 'It's incredibly detailed.'

'It's a geo map. The couloir I'll be riding in a couple of days. We're doing a film, promoting a board…' He felt shy suddenly. 'It's a board I had a hand in designing so it's kind of a big deal.'

She twisted her head. 'You're a designer too?' And then she was giggling. 'No wonder you have to pack in the protein.'

He felt a jolt in his belly, laughter starting. 'You saw that, huh?'

She was wide smiling. 'It's your best role yet! I went straight out to buy that yoghurt!'

She was too lovely. All sparkling eyes and alluring neckline. But it wasn't just that. She was interested in the map, and in the descent that he was planning. It meant a lot.

'I made that advert back in my competition days. I don't advertise that stuff any more.' He tore his eyes away from hers and leaned over to move the mouse, hovering the cursor over a point at the summit. 'So…the helicopter will drop me here…'

'Helicopter?' The chair spun and his pulse spiked. She was looking up at him, giving him a bird's-eye view down the front of her blouse.

Milky throat, collarbones, breasts cupped in dark lace.

He swallowed hard. 'I have to ride the line over and over so the camera crew can take different angles. A helicopter's the quickest way to get me back to the top.'

She grimaced a bit. 'I find helicopters terrifying!'

'Like the luge was terrifying?'

Her lips parted for a beat and then she smiled. 'Well, maybe I'm growing! Today, I went on a ride suitable for three-year-olds. In twenty years, who knows? I might graduate to helicopters!'

He couldn't not put a hand to her cheek. 'I'd like to be there to see that.'

Something came and went behind her eyes, and then she was rising up, sliding her arms around his neck, her gaze reaching right in, taking him all apart. 'I think we should start our date now.'

He felt a tingle starting. 'What do you want to do?'

A smile touched the corners of her mouth. 'I think you know.'

She nestled into Dax's firm warmth, smiling inside. She couldn't make herself regret this, even though it was the anniversary of André's death, even though the geo map of the couloir had stirred a dread in her belly that she'd had to hide. Right now, Dax was here, safe, in her bed and in her heart. Deep in. Secretly. She ran her fingers over his chest. Smooth. Contoured in all the right places. Was she deep in his heart too, secretly? Was that what she'd seen in his eyes when he'd said that thing about wanting to be there in twenty years to see her braving a helicopter...? Only he knew, but she'd felt something, something that had stopped her breath and drawn her to her feet.

His hand suddenly covered hers, squeezing softly. 'Are you all right?'

How couldn't he know? She hadn't held anything back, wouldn't have been able to even if she'd tried. She shifted so she could see his face. 'What would you guess?'

His eyebrows drew in. 'I think, maybe...yes...'

'Then you're right!'

'Good!' His eyes crinkled. 'I like to be sure.'

'I've noticed.'

A shadow flitted across his face. 'Does it annoy you, me asking all the time?'

'No. I just sometimes wonder how you can't tell.'

For a beat, his face stiffened, and then he sighed. 'That would be down to Colette. She messed me up good!'

She felt her stomach tightening. She had a low enough opinion of his mother already, not being 'hands-on', not helping him with Yann, not remembering his favourite toys, letting him leave home at sixteen. *Sixteen!* What else was left for her to have screwed up?

She wriggled out of his arms, settling herself on her side. 'Do you want to talk about it?'

'Not really.' He turned his head, trapping her in a pained gaze, and then he was rolling over to face her. 'Colette's flaky, okay. As a kid, I never knew whether I was in or out.' His voice cracked a little. 'The worst thing was, she could change in a heartbeat, go from sweet and smiling to not, and I'd think it was my fault, that I'd caused it.' His focus seemed to turn inwards. 'If I'd had a father around, to balance it out, maybe...'

She felt tears thickening in her throat, burning behind her eyes. André's parents had changed in a heartbeat too, but she'd only had to endure the pain once, as an adult, not over and over again as a child.

He sighed. 'I got in the habit of trying to pre-empt her, asking if she was all right, and I'd keep asking, just to be sure, because if she was all right—'

'Then it meant you could feel okay too.' She swallowed hard. He was breaking her heart.

He nodded slowly. 'I could never work out if she loved me. Sometimes she'd look at me as if she did, but then...' He shrugged. 'By the time I got to my teens, I was sick of being on the receiving end. I turned bad, cut school all the time to go skateboarding. I wanted to wind her up, get to her...'

'No, you didn't.' His eyes went silent. 'You wanted her to say stop.'

He looked at her for a long second and then he blinked. 'Deep down, I suppose that's what I was doing, yes. If she'd stopped me, it would have meant she cared but she never said a word.' He took a breath and then a smile touched his lips. 'The silver lining was that I got really good at skateboarding, which made moving to snow-boarding a breeze, and that was good because from the moment I put my feet into those bind-ings my life started making sense.' His eyes were filling with light. 'Everything felt right. I was in my element. I won competitions. Got no-ticed. I went from being a rich entitled brat with "issues" to being a respected sportsman and as long as I kept delivering on the slopes, as long as I kept myself at the top of the game, the ben-efits flowed in. Sponsorship, travel, friends... yoghurt adverts! After Colette, it was liberating. No second-guessing. No wondering if I was in or out. I knew exactly what I had to do to earn my place.'

Earn your place! She took a needle to the heart. On the slopes Dax looked so powerful, so self-assured, but on the inside, he was absolutely not all right, and all because of Colette! She swallowed hard. 'Is Colette proud of you now? Does she watch you? Your films?' *Does she know the risks you take?* She could hear the bitter edge in her voice. 'Does she ever visit?'

He shook his head. 'I don't know what she thinks, and no, she doesn't visit. Colette hates Cham. She's not a snow person.'

Not a mother, not a grandmother, not a support, not a helpmate, and now, conveniently, not a snow person. Colette was blessed with a beautiful son, and a beautiful grandson. How couldn't she see it, how couldn't she love them?

'Hey!' He was frowning. 'Are you all right?'

'No, actually…' She sat up, heart trembling, tears thickening in her throat. 'I can't stand it, Dax, hearing about Colette… The way she is, the way she's been, not caring about you, not helping, not caring about Yann…'

He was rolling up, putting his hands on her shoulders, taking her apart with his eyes. 'Simone, baby, where's all this coming from?'

'From bitter experience…' She clamped her eyes shut, trying to stop her tears spilling out, but it was no good, they were winding down her cheeks with all the hate and pain she had inside. She swallowed hard, meeting his gaze. 'I know how it *feels*, Dax, that's why I'm raging.' Her chest was exploding, debris flying. 'After André died, my in-laws turned on me and Chloe without warning! I'd thought they were decent people, but they shut their door on us. On *Chloe*, for God's sake, their own granddaughter! *Why?* I just can't get my head around it. My in-laws! Your mother! Behaving, like, I don't know what! What's *wrong* with them all?'

'I don't know.' His eyes were reaching in, clouding, and then his hands tightened on her shoulders. 'What do you mean, they *turned* on you?'

'They blamed me!' Suddenly, her throat was full of dust. 'For everything!'

He shifted, pulling the duvet up around her, and then his eyes were on hers again. 'Breathe, and then talk...'

His gaze was warm, bolstering. She wiped her face, then inhaled slowly, feeling her pulse slowing, moisture softening her mouth. 'André's parents are wealthy. He was an only child, their only focus. He was a violinist, like me, but super talented. His parents had thrown a lot at tuition. They were *invested*, had high expectations, and he did too. He wanted to be first violin in the Paris Orchestra...

'We were students when we met. Just before we graduated, I found out I was pregnant.' Dax's eyebrows flickered. 'We were shocked, but we were in love, so we got married. My in-laws helped us with money, paid the rent on a decent apartment. André kept on with his music. I looked after Chloe, and, when I could, I played with a string quartet, to keep my hand in. And then…it happened.' She felt her breath stalling, her eyes prickling again. 'He was carrying Chloe's Christmas present across the road when the car struck him. A huge box. A doll's house we'd picked out for her…'

Dax took her hands, folding them into his, his eyes searching. 'I still don't see—'

'Why would you?' She felt a fresh wave of anger building. 'There's no logic! His parents came unhinged, needed to blame someone and that someone was me. It went like this: I got pregnant on purpose to trap André into marrying me because… I was a gold-digger!'

His mouth fell open. 'No!'

'Oh, it gets worse.' His eyes narrowed. 'They said that if André hadn't had a child, he'd never have been on that crossing with that child's Christmas present…*that child*, thank you very much!' She couldn't stop now, her words coming, her tears flowing, everything pouring out. 'They cut us off, turned their backs. They won't see Chloe and I just can't…' She gulped down a breath. 'I just *can't* understand. She's so, so beautiful…a piece of André right there that they could be cherishing. Why don't they love her? Why don't they want her in their lives?'

Dax was shaking his head. 'Oh, Simone.' And then his arms were going around her, and she was melting into him, letting it all out, and he was holding her tight and close, stroking her hair and, after how long she couldn't tell, she felt the grip of her anger loosening, and her pain was flowing away, flowing, and flowing, and suddenly there was room to breathe, light streaming in.

Maybe he sensed it because suddenly he was nuzzling her hair. 'Why didn't you go home?'

She eased herself out of his arms, meeting his warm, brown gaze. 'I don't know... Maybe deep down, I didn't want to feel like I'd been defeated. I love my parents, but I'd always dreamed of living in Paris. I wanted to take Chloe to André's favourite places, talk about the things he'd loved, so she'd feel him more, so he wouldn't be just a face in a photograph.'

'Keeping him alive for her, like you told me to do with Zara...'

She nodded. 'It seemed even more important after what her grandparents did.' She drew in a slow breath, looking into his face. Melting gaze. Dark, dark lashes. That perfect mouth. So handsome! Talking was good, sharing things was good, but she was tired of talking now. She rose up onto her knees, letting the quilt fall, taking his face in her hands, running the tip of her nose along his. 'Are you all right, Dax?'

His eyebrows flashed. 'I think I'm about to be.'

She felt a smile coming. 'I think you could be right.'

CHAPTER ELEVEN

December 20th...

'LAST RUN, DAX.' Pierre's voice was crackling in his ear. 'Make it count!'

'Don't I always?'

'Negative!' Pierre was chuckling. 'Your last run sucked!'

He felt a smile coming. 'Take a hike, slacker!' Pierre goading him was normal. It was what they did, winding each other up, but he just wanted to get going. 'Look, I'm ready! Set me free, man.'

'Hang on—' Pierre's voice dropped out, then came back. 'Sorry, Dax. Take five, Axel's got an issue with the drone.'

His stomach dived. He was loose, raring to go. Waiting was a buzzkill! He sighed into the microphone. 'Copy that.'

He slid back six inches and pushed up his goggles. Big sky, wide vista, splintered peaks...

This was his world, his stomach-clenching, heart-thumping world. He inhaled, long and slow. Yann thought he was fearless, watched his films over and over. He was always asking questions, admiration burning in his eyes. Dax felt his chest filling. Being admired by Yann felt huge. *Massive!* It crowned him king, made him feel like a real *papa*! But he wasn't fearless. His nerves were chiming as always, but that was fine. He knew the score, knew where he stood with the mountain. It was an honest relationship like…like the one he was miraculously having with Simone. *Him!* In a proper relationship! His chest filled again, fit to burst. It was insane, the way he felt around Simone. The best kind of dizzy…and special. She made him *feel* special. When she looked at him with that sweet light in her eyes, he actually felt taller. *Cherished!*

It was new, feeling cared for, and…caring in return. Feeling torn in two over what she'd been through with her in-laws. *Unbelievable!* And yet, no more unbelievable than what he had to endure at his mother's hands. He swallowed. So much hurt, so many scars… When Simone had told him last night how she'd had to sell her violin to help make ends meet, he'd felt actual relief, a giddy buzz of anticipation. A departed violin was something he could fix!

Static crackled in his ear and he flinched,

coming to. Standing at the top of the mountain not thinking about the mountain was new as well. *Focus!* He scanned the slope, running his hands over his harness, tightening straps. He looked at the tracks from his previous rides, the little deviations he'd made each time, playing with the powder, innovating. He felt his pulse gathering. There was nothing like the tingling anticipation of riding a pristine slope, senses taut on high alert, the rush that came from riding into the unknown, but riding a tested slope, flying the same line over and over again was a different kind of blast. It was all about fun, and speed, and exhilaration!

'Dax!'

'Pierre!' He pushed his earpiece against his ear. 'Are we good?'

'Almost. The drone's up.'

He pulled his goggles down, letting his eyes adjust, then he coasted to the edge. The drone was rising, drawing level, and then it was above his head, hovering like a curious insect. His pulse spiked, adrenaline kicking in. He took a breath: 'I'm ready!'

Pierre's voice filled his ear. 'Go on five, four, three, two, *one*!'

He rocked back then launched himself over the edge, feeling the snow, finding his rhythm, owning the board, working it, weaving tight zigzags, spraying pow on the turns. Yann loved seeing him spray the powder. *Yann!* His six-year-old speed-freak son! He seemed to have a sense for the board, knew how to use his weight, how to move. He was already at home on the baby slopes, getting more and more confident. Yann was a natural!

He ducked his knees, crouching to touch the snow just for the pure joy of it, and then he was out of the couloir, emerging onto a wide, white expanse. *Playtime!* The tracks he'd left before were crumbling, blurring. *Track away!* He carved left, leaning hard, loving the way the pow was flying. Time to straighten, ride like the wind, take the spur head on…three-sixty spin, quick board grab. *Yes!* Crushing it!

Simone had asked him how he didn't get dizzy. A high cry tore from his mouth involuntarily as happiness crammed his heart. *Simone!* Turning three sixty in the air at fifty kilometres an hour didn't make him dizzy in the slightest, but she did. It only took one look, a flicker of one eyebrow, a single feather touch of her finger to turn him inside out and upside down. He felt heat tingling in his veins. He wanted her, wanted her as he'd never wanted anyone before. As soon as he got back, he was going to steal her away, take her to his room, lay her down and unwrap her… He could already hear her sighs, smell the warm musk of her. *Oh, God!* He was going to take her lips, then trail kisses down her throat, all the way to—

'Avalanche!' Pierre's frantic shout filled his ears, emptying his lungs. *'Get out of there, Dax!'*

He looked down, saw snow shifting under snow, coming alive. *Get out!* He felt his heart exploding in slow motion, then everything sped up. The snow was shaking, throwing him sideways, boiling and rumbling, and then it struck his back, bowling him forwards. He gasped, floundering, and then he remembered what he had to do to stand a chance. *ABS!* He yanked the strap, felt the balloon swelling around his neck and head. *Stay on top!* He covered his nose and mouth with his arm, sucked in a breath, then fought with his other arm, striking for the light. He broke the surface for a nanosecond, but then something hard socked him in the back, and he was floundering again, gagging. *Cover your nose and mouth!* He screwed his eyes shut, giving in to the drag and tumble, cartwheeling, over and over. He was boneless, like Chloe's monkey, what was he called…? *Serge!* That was it: Serge. And Yann's panda was Maurice. How could he ever forget Maurice? Lost in the airport. At least he'd found Maurice. Would he be found? *Yes!* He was wearing his tracker. It would show them where to dig… *No! No! No!*

He wasn't dying. *Couldn't* die. Yann needed him. Simone and Chloe needed him. He had to fight, *had* to get back to the surface. He couldn't let all of Simone's worst nightmares come true. He couldn't. He wasn't giving up.

He blinked, trying to focus through the thundering whiteness. *There!* Brighter patches. That was the top! He lifted his arms, heavy, heavy arms. His body was being dragged, flayed by the mountain, but if he didn't get to the light, he'd be buried alive. No air. No chance of surviving. Snow set like concrete when it stopped moving, everyone knew that.

He struck upwards, arm over arm, clawing at snow and air, then air and snow, powered by adrenaline and sheer will. His muscles were screaming, but he wasn't broken. He was winning, moving up, arm over arm, fighting and then he felt the rush and rumble slowing. *No!* His pulse spiked. He tore at the snow, lunging towards the light, dragging himself upwards, driving his body forwards. One last push before the snow clamped his legs and pinned his arms. One last push! And then there was the blue, blue sky, and air to breathe, and the frantic thumping of his still beating heart.

'Scampy Dog is so funny!' Chloe was leaning against her, giggling hard. On her other side,

Yann was chuckling, bumping her with his shoulder as he jounced.

She looked at the screen, trying to engage, but it was no good. Dax was out, making his film, the one that needed the helicopter, and it was all she could think about. When he'd been building up his snow fitness, sticking to the re-sorts, it had been easier to relax. The resorts had safety crews and constant avalanche moni-toring. But now he was riding the steep couloir she'd seen on his computer screen with only a film crew and helicopter pilot to hand, and her faith in him and in his sense for the mountain seemed to be deserting her.

She felt her ribs tightening. This was the re-ality of caring for Dax, of *loving* him. Feeling that low hum of anxiety thrumming through her veins, dreading the worst when he was out, feeling massive relief and boundless happiness whenever he was safe and near. Three days ago she'd told herself that no matter how compli-cated things were, she was ready to take a risk on Dax. She'd thrown caution to the wind, told him she cared about him, but was she really up to coping with this gnawing fear? Was this re-lationship really doable?

Dax! Always stopping her breath, or making it catch. He could do it with just a look, with the slightest touch. From the moment he'd kissed her in the snow, she'd been walking on air, feeling something real and wonderful taking flight. Every time they made love, or talked into the night, she felt closer to him, more deeply attached, and that was making it harder to bear the thought of anything happening to him. But what could she do? In the woods she'd told Dax she *cared* about him because it had felt too soon to talk about love. They were brand new! And if it was too soon to be telling him that she was in love with him, then it was too soon to be making demands, asking him to stop doing the thing he loved, the thing that had turned his life around, given him a sense of self-worth, a feeling of earning his place. As if he even had to *earn* his place… But how to tell him that, without it sounding as if she was trying to control him, change him!

She looked at Yann. She'd hoped that *he* would be the key…that *he* would be the one to make Dax rethink things, but it was Yann who'd changed, Yann who'd come out of his shell and become Dax's biggest fan. Mobbing Dax when he came in, wanting to hear every last detail of his runs, how much air he'd got, how many somersaults he'd turned. Hero worship! To think Dax had sat in that bistro telling her he couldn't connect with his son! They were well and truly connected now.

Snowboarding buddies! But Yann only saw the glory. He didn't see the danger. And neither did Chloe. She loved being out on her board with Dax, and Dax was so good with her. So gentle, so patient. He was so good with both of them, a natural teacher! Exacting, meticulous—*of course*—but always making things fun. She felt a sudden warmth pulsing through her heart. Dax had so much to give, and he gave it in spades, all the time. If only he would stop putting himself in danger...

She blinked, looking at the screen again, feeling her toes curling. The movie was banal and there was another hour to go. She couldn't! She needed some air, maybe a walk around the veranda.

She extricated herself from the stew of arms and legs. 'Listen, you two, Scampy Dog isn't doing it for me.' She got to her feet. 'I'm going upstairs for a bit.'

'Okay.' Chloe didn't take her eyes off the screen.

Yann glanced up, shot her a little smile, then seeped into the space she'd left, leaning his shoulder against Chloe's.

She smiled. 'If you need anything, Chantal's in the kitchen.'

Two heads nodded.

She slipped from the room, crossing the hall,

but then suddenly her feet turned to clay. Dax was sitting on the stairs, shoulders slumped, head bent.

Her heart pulsed. This wasn't him! He always came to find them when he got back, always came bounding in high as a kite. She forced her feet to move, closing the distance between them, heart going. 'Dax? Are you all right?'

He blinked, his face pale as paper, and then something raw filled his eyes, something that made her breath catch. 'I am now.' And then he was getting to his feet, grabbing her hand, pulling her up the stairs, going fast.

She didn't try to resist. He was in the grip of something, and she needed to know what it was. At the top of the stairs he caught her eye for a beat and then he was pulling her along again, powerful shoulders shifting under his shirt. At her bedroom door he turned, speaking in low tones. 'Where are the kids?'

'Watching a movie.'

'How long?' His gaze was molten, openly carnal.

Her pulse spiked. 'About an hour.'

'Good.' He leaned in, brushing her lips with his, and then he was tugging her on, past Yann's room and into his, kicking the door shut behind them. When his eyes came back to hers, she could see heat and hunger, and something else too, hiding in the shadows, a haunted look that was tearing at her heart.

'Dax… What's wrong?'

'Nothing.' He was moving in close. She felt his hands on her waist, his lips in her hair. She closed her eyes, breathing him in, fighting the dizziness she always felt around him. And then his hands were sliding under her sweater, caressing her skin in warm waves, his fingers travelling the length of her spine to her nape. She felt her pulse jump, heat rising, but around the edges of it she could feel anxiety shimmering. Dax was a confident lover, always passionate, but this was different. *He* was different.

She put her hands on his chest, pushing back. 'Dax…?' She looked up, trying to see past the heat in his eyes. 'There is something. Tell me.'

He blinked, his gaze clearing for a moment, and then he was shaking his head, his voice low, strangled-sounding. 'I just want you, okay. I want to feel you close…' A smile ghosted tightly on his lips. 'Isn't that enough?'

Her heart pulsed, then she felt it flowing out to him in waves. There was something going on, pain behind the desperate need burning in his eyes and she wanted to take it away, make him better. Suddenly it was the only thing that mattered.

She slid her hands up and around his neck,

stroking his nape, looking into his face. 'Yes, it's enough.'

He made a low noise in his throat, and then his lips were scorching hers, igniting a fire in her veins, turning her insides to liquid.

'You're so beautiful.' Dax was trailing kisses along her collarbone.

Her chest panged softly. What had just happened between them had emptied her out. She felt deliciously used. Boneless! He'd loved her hard, consumed her to the last drop. She was feeling the best kind of dizzy, but she couldn't forget that he'd been sitting on the stairs, pale as paper.

She put her hand to his face, stroking his cheek, sliding her thumb into the sandpaper zone. 'Are you all right?'

He lifted his head, a hazy smile in his eyes. 'You've stolen my line.'

Smiling Dax! She felt her own lips curving up. 'I'm only borrowing it because "I have to pack in the protein" isn't such a good fit.'

He chuckled softly. 'But actually it is...' He fell to nuzzling her neck, trailing more kisses. 'That was quite the workout!'

'Yes, it was.' She ran her fingers over the swell of his shoulder, steeling herself. 'Are you going to tell me why?'

His head came up and then his lips were on hers, teasing softly. 'Because you're irresistible. Because I can't get enough of you.'

Was he being deliberately disingenuous? She caught his face in her hands, easing him back. 'I want to know why you didn't come into the den when you got back. Why were you sitting on the stairs?'

A shadow crossed his face, and then he was rolling away, sitting up. 'How long have we been up here?'

Did he really think avoiding the question was going to work? She levered herself up, ready to pursue, but then her breath stopped. There was a livid bruise low down on his back, purple shadows ghosting around it. 'Dax!' She moved closer, felt her pulse quickening. 'What the hell happened? You're all bruised.'

He stiffened, and then he was turning himself round slowly. His face was paper again, his eyes two holes punched through. He licked his lips. 'Avalanche...'

A memory pulsed. His film...that slab cracking behind him as he'd traversed the snowfield... vertical lines fizzing either side as he'd been flying down. He'd kept ahead, and the snow hadn't come after him, not that time, but today...

She couldn't hold his gaze, couldn't breathe. What had happened to his sixth sense? She'd been wound tight with nerves all afternoon, but she'd *wanted* to believe in it, *needed* to believe in it! But now she could feel her faith shattering and ugly words crowding onto her tongue. She bit them back. Blowing her stack wasn't going to help. He didn't need *I told you so*. He knew well enough. Of course he did. That was the dark smudge she'd seen behind his eyes. She inhaled slowly, steadying herself. He was alive. That was the main thing, the thing to hold onto. But he was in shock, bruised. His confidence all dented. Right now, he needed kindness.

'Oh, Dax...' She wrapped her arms around him, felt him softening against her, holding on tight. She pressed her lips to his neck, breathing him in, stroking his hair. 'What happened?'

'I don't know...' His breath was ragged. 'It happened so fast. One second I was flying... The next, all hell broke loose. The slab...came... alive. Before I could do anything, I was caught... being dragged... The bruise must have been a rock. I remember.' She felt his body shuddering. 'I thought I was going to die.' Suddenly he was pulling away, looking into her eyes. 'I was so lucky, Sim. So, so lucky!'

She felt tears thickening in her throat. Lucky was an understatement! Her worst nightmare had almost come true, having to tell Yann that his *papa* was dead...but this wasn't only about

Yann now. It was bigger. She'd let it get bigger. Falling for Dax, letting Chloe fall for Dax… *Chloe!* Letting her cuddle up to him at bedtimes…letting her get close to Dax… *Oh, God!* What had she done?

'Hey!' He was looking at her, a gleam coming into his eyes, and then he was folding her into his arms, pulling her against his chest. 'I'm still here.' His lips grazed her forehead. 'We're all right.'

Were they all right? Could they be? He *was* still here, warm and breathing, holding her close. It was what happened next that mattered. That was the thing! He knew how close he'd come. Maybe it would all work out for the best. This could be a wake-up call, especially if she underlined it.

She shifted backwards, holding his arms. 'You're still here, yes, but what about tomorrow, and the next day, and the day after that? What about Aiguille du Plan?' Something came and went behind his eyes, and then he was going pale again, the corners of his mouth tightening. She felt a prick of guilt. She didn't want to be piling on pressure when the bruises were so fresh, but she had a stake in his life now, and so did Chloe. As for Yann… Her heart panged. Yann *needed* his *papa.* She swallowed hard. She *had* to pin Dax down, for all their sakes. She looked into his eyes, holding fast. 'What are you going to do, Dax, going forward?'

For a long second, he held her gaze, and then his hand cupped her cheek, and he was stroking her cheekbone with a soft thumb, his eyes dark and liquid. 'I'm not going to die, Sim.' His lips parted for a beat. 'I'm going to have to reappraise.'

'What does that mean?'

He reached for her, pulling her in again, and she felt his lips in her hair, his breath tingling through. 'It means Aiguille du Plan is off.'

She closed her eyes, feeling wetness welling behind them, relief streaming through her veins. He was safe, was going to stay safe! She clung to him, heart filling and filling, but then he was shifting, putting her from him gently, leaning to retrieve their clothes from the floor.

'We should go down before they send out a search party.'

She looked at the purple island on his back. 'Are you going to tell Yann?'

He stiffened momentarily, and then he was pulling on his shirt. 'No. I couldn't...' He seemed to falter, and then he turned. 'I'm not sure if we'll put the film out or not, but if we do, I'll talk to him about it then.'

Her heart panged. Of course, Pierre must have filmed the whole thing. She shuddered. It wasn't a film she ever wanted to see! She pulled on her sweater. 'Did you get checked by a medic?'

'Of course.' He stood up, tucking in his shirt. 'Superficial injury! They said I was lucky.' And then he smiled, stealing her breath away. 'But we know that, right!'

CHAPTER TWELVE

December 22nd...

'HEY, DAX, HOW are you doing?'

Guilt panged in his chest. Pierre had called him yesterday too, but he hadn't been in the mood for talking. He'd been in a dip, feeling blue, which was crazy because shouldn't he have been feeling high on life? He'd survived an avalanche! Life should have been tasting sweet, but for some reason he was up one minute, down the next, churning away inside, feeling the pull of a hundred threads.

'I'm okay.' He dug out an upbeat tone. 'Sorry, I didn't call back. I was with the kids.'

'That's cool. Where are you, man? I'm picking up an outdoor vibe.'

'At ski school, watching the kids.' He moved along the rail to a quiet spot. 'Yann likes me to see how he's coming along, although he prefers his snowboard.'

'No surprise! His *papa* is the boss!'

His chest went tight. Boss of what? Messing up?

Pierre's voice was downshifting. 'Seriously though…are you okay?'

He felt a judder inside, something collapsing. 'I don't know.' He blew out a sigh. 'I'm all over the place, to be honest.'

'That's allowed. It was scary. It's okay to be feeling shaken.' Pierre paused, a functional sort of pause, as if he was sipping something. 'You should have gone back up, Dax.'

He closed his eyes, felt his gut twisting. It was what he'd been telling himself for the past twenty-four hours. He should have ridden the line again, pegged his fear right back into its hole. Getting caught by the avalanche had spooked him, but aside from the bruising he'd been fine, more than capable of going again. If he had, he could have gone home triumphant, able to face Yann, instead of skulking on the stairs, feeling like a failure. But straight after, his heart had been beating only for Simone and Yann and Chloe. All he'd wanted was to get back to them, not risk another run, just in case.

Simone's words had collected themselves around him: *I don't want to be the one who has to tell Yannick that his papa thought riding a snowboard down a cliff was more important than being a father...'* And in the afterglow of spared life, he'd felt the full weight of them, had felt that nothing on earth was more important than his little Christmas family. Being with them, not doing anything to hurt them.

He sighed. 'Maybe.'

'You did everything right, *everything*! You didn't panic. That's why you came through. You should be proud of yourself!'

Proud? Yes, he'd remembered his avalanche drill, but before launching, when he should have been casing the terrain, he'd been thinking about Yann, feeling buzzed about the way Yann worshipped him. And then he'd been thinking about Simone, thinking about how wonderful it was having someone he could talk to properly...and just before the avalanche had struck, when he should have been concentrating on the snow, paying attention, he'd been fantasising about undressing her. That was why he hadn't noticed paradise turning to hell right under his board, why Pierre's frantic warning had given him such a jolt.

'Dax?'

'Sorry! Chloe took a tumble but she's all right.' It was a lie, but it would do. It was good of Pierre to be boosting him like this, but he couldn't cope with a full debrief. His head was cluttering, and his insides were twisting themselves into knots. He was a mess!

'It's fine…' Pierre paused. 'I was just wondering what you're thinking…about Aiguille du Plan?'

Dax's chest panged. He'd told Simone Aiguille du Plan was off, but he hadn't quite got around to telling Pierre yet. He hadn't had the chance. The previous day he'd been non-stop with the kids, then with other stuff, something driving him like a piston, keeping him going until he'd been wiped out. But he could tell Pierre now, couldn't he? Put it to bed, the line he'd been obsessing about for over a year, the line he'd come back to Cham to make his own, the line Yann had wanted to see on the computer over and over again, the line that made Yann's eyes ignite and burn…

He took a breath. 'I don't know, Pierre. Right now, I can't even think straight.'

'It's cool, man. I'm not bringing it up to push you. I'd never do that. It's your call. You've got to feel a hundred per cent.' Pierre paused. 'All I wanted to say is that the conditions are looking good for Christmas Eve…'

Simone shivered into her jacket, sipping her coffee. Sitting inside would have been warmer, but the outdoor tables with their jolly red chairs, flickering pavement heaters and little Christmas trees dotted about had looked so appealing. Besides, she'd been hoping that the happy bustling crowds and the gaily adorned horse traps going past would lift her spirits, but somehow they were only making her feel worse.

She set her cup down, feeling the knots in her stomach tightening. She ought to have been walking on air. Dax had survived an avalanche! He'd ditched Aiguille du Plan. He'd said he was reappraising. It was everything she'd wanted, for Yann, for herself and for Chloe, but something wasn't right. With him.

Yesterday, he'd coached Yann and Chloe on their boards until they'd been dead on their feet. Then he'd waxed the cars to within an inch of their lives. After the kids had gone to bed, he'd lapped the pool for over an hour then fallen asleep on the sofa. She'd watched him for a while, then covered him with a throw, thinking he'd come to her room when he woke up, but he hadn't. First thing that morning he'd had the kids out on their boards again, and now he was at the ski school. He was still smiling but there was something missing.

She picked up her cup and put it down again without drinking. It wasn't what she'd been expecting. Yes, he'd taken a knock, not just physically—although *that* didn't seem to be slowing him down any—but psychologically too. He had to have been wondering about his sixth sense, feeling shattered about the way it had failed him, but even so, *even so*, surely staring death in the face and coming out the other side should have been making him shine more brightly, should have been making him just... more! But instead, he seemed less, not on the outside, but somewhere behind his eyes, and she couldn't stop thinking about it.

She slid her cup away. Maybe she was expecting too much. The avalanche had only happened two days ago. He was probably still in shock. Maybe all his non-stop motion was just him trying to outrun what had happened in some way...

Probably...? Maybe...?

The thing was, she didn't actually know—

'Madame?' A young man was putting a flier down on her table.

She watched him weaving through the tables, handing out fliers, feeling an ache tearing at her chest. The problem was Dax wasn't talking to her about it. If he'd come to her room last night, if he'd slipped in beside her, all warm, talking into the night as they'd done before, she wouldn't have been churning away like this. Two days ago, he'd towed her up the stairs and loved her as if she'd been life itself, but since then, it had almost felt as if he was keeping her

at a distance. *Why?* She felt tears prickling at
the edges of her eyes. She was here for him,
wanted to help him through it, but he wasn't
giving her a chance.

Yet...

She drew in a long breath, wiping her eyes.
Maybe this was *her* hang-up, not Dax's, because
she wanted him to turn to her, not only for sex,
but for all the love she had inside, the love she
hadn't declared yet but wanted to. She wanted to
flow into his spaces, fill him up, be his everything. And because it wasn't working out that
way—*yet*—she was getting stupidly insecure.
For pity's sake! Just because he hadn't come to
her last night didn't mean he was pushing her
away. Maybe he simply hadn't wanted to disturb
her! And he'd hadn't crashed on the sofa to upset
her, but because he'd worn himself out, and he'd
worn himself out because it was his way of dealing with what he'd been through, which was,
after all, a pretty big deal. She needed to get a
grip. Stop being so sensitive!

She looked along the street, noticing the time
on the pretty little clock tower. The other thing
she needed was not to be wasting her afternoon. Dax had told her to take some time out,
hit the spa, anything she wanted, but what she
wanted, what she *really* wanted was to find him
a Christmas present even though he'd made her

promise not to. She felt warmth rising inside. How could he ever have thought she'd be able to keep a promise like that?

The problem was Dax had everything already!

She went for her cup but then the flier caught her eye. *The Alpine Museum!* She snatched it up. An entire museum devoted to Alpinism in Chamonix! There was bound to be a gift shop. She scanned the leaflet, felt her pulse quickening. There was a temporary photo exhibition. *Perfect!* Dax had that huge photo of Mont Blanc on his office wall! Maybe there'd be something there that could work as a companion, assuming the gift shop was stocking repro prints, and if it didn't, she could always look online. A black and white mountain landscape would be perfect!

She gathered up her things, suddenly feeling light as air. Going on a mission was way better than moping. The museum was bound to be interesting, and it might just turn up a surprise!

She glanced at her watch and gasped. Had she really been in the museum for over an hour already? She hadn't meant to get distracted, but the place was simply too fascinating. The history of the early climbers and mountaineers who'd gone up Mont Blanc had been captivating. And the gear! Light years away from the fancy kit Dax had. Wooden skis and poles, unwieldy long-handled ice axes and picks, jute ropes. And the clothes…nothing lightweight and properly waterproof. All woollen…jackets and plus fours, socks, and hats.

She scooted through the geological exhibition, sliding her eyes over the huge lumps of glittering quartz, but she couldn't not stop to look at the stuffed wolf. Grey with yellow eyes. Right up Chloe and Yann's street!

Finally she came to the photo exhibition: *Walking Through Mountain Time*. She felt a tingle shimmering between her shoulder blades. Surely, there'd be something here for Dax. She drew in a breath and stepped into the dark hall, feeling its reverential hush wrapping itself around her.

The first images were black and white. Crisp, imposing landscapes. Stiffly posed pioneering mountaineers and blurrier group photos of early tourists with smiles and sticks and canvas packs. She walked on, going slowly. It really was like walking through time, seeing the mountains change, the Savoie glacier shrinking, the town growing. Along the next row, there were colour photographs, action shots of skiers and mountaineers, but there was nothing for Dax. She moved on, turning the corner into the next exhibition space and then her breath stopped. In front of her was a huge picture of a thundering avalanche. She shuddered. Dax had said that his avalanche had been mercifully small by avalanche standards. This one wasn't. She looked at it for a long moment, feeling its immensity. Definitely not the right picture to give him.

She tore her eyes away, turning to the accompanying panel of smaller photographs, captioned *Mont Blanc avalanche claims record number of lives*. She looked along the row of pictures feeling a sick ache clawing at her stomach. Crews digging for bodies. Grave-faced mountain rescue teams. A hovering helicopter. And then, her mouth turned to dust. Dax was staring out of one of the pictures.

Dax!

She swallowed hard. It couldn't be Dax! It was a mistake! *Clearly!* They must have made a mistake. She leaned in close, holding her breath. It *was* him! Standing with a line of smiling men holding skis. *Skis?* Dax didn't ski! She scanned the caption underneath the picture, blinking away the spots that were suddenly dancing in front of her eyes.

World champion free skier Camille Deuzlier and support team perish in Mont Blanc avalanche.

She put her hand out, steadying herself against the cabinet. Not Dax, then. *No!* Of course not! Dax was alive. He was with Chloe and Yann. But if it wasn't Dax… Her pulse quickened, started roaring in her ears. She sucked in a breath, forcing herself to look at the date over the main avalanche picture again and suddenly she could feel a sob rising, filling her throat. The dates tallied. Dax was twenty-nine. The man in the picture had died thirty years ago. Could it be…could it possibly somehow be that the man in the picture with Camille Deuzlier was Dax's father?

She sank onto the step outside, breathing hard, and then she looked at the photo she'd taken with her phone. The man was the spit of Dax, or, rather, Dax was the spit of him! It *had* to be Dax's father! But who was he? She typed 'Camille Deuzlier' into her phone with trembling fingers. *There!* Same photo, but with an article. She skimmed, looking for the names of Deuzlier's team, clicking links. *There!* That was him: Gabriel Dax Guillot. Dax's father! Found!

She took a screenshot, then rolled her phone over and over in her hands. Gabriel had died on Mont Blanc thirty years ago. Two days ago, Dax had nearly succumbed to the same fate. Whatever crazy thing it was that drew Dax to the mountain, it clearly ran in the blood. Nature, not nurture! Maybe that was why he'd always felt that the mountains were his natural home. Maybe that was why his son seemed to have been born to ride a snowboard!

She drew in a slow breath, running her eyes over the jagged peaks that rose, towering over the town. What now? Should she tell Dax? Would telling him be meddling in something that was none of her business? After all, Colette had hidden his father's identity from Dax for a reason. But what reason? She closed her eyes. Unless…unless reason had nothing to do with it. Hadn't Dax said that his mother hated Chamonix? Maybe Colette hated Chamonix because Mont Blanc had taken the man she loved. The date on the picture…? She must have been pregnant when the avalanche happened. Had she gone back to Paris, had her baby, seen Gabriel in him and hadn't been able to bear it? Was that why she'd blown hot and cold with Dax his whole life, one side of her wanting to love him, the other side being too scared to in case he was torn away from her too? Hardly credible, but if that was Colette's reality then maybe it didn't have to make sense to anyone but her, any more than André's parents' attitude to Chloe didn't make sense. She swallowed hard. It was twisted sense. Warped logic. Misguided. *Wrong!* But maybe that was what grief did to some people.

She felt a shiver fingering her spine. The gift of his father's identity, and tragic fate, wasn't exactly the surprise she'd had in mind for Dax. She couldn't tell him now, not when he was dealing with his own avalanche trauma. She needed him to come right first. Until then, she'd have to keep it to herself.

CHAPTER THIRTEEN

December 23rd...

DAX KILLED THE engine and slumped back on the seat of the snowmobile. He twisted, testing his body, trying to find a patch of pain, but nothing was twinging. Not around the bruise site anyway. All the twinging was happening on the inside, torment pulling him all apart.

He drew in a long breath, felt his heart panging over and over.

What was wrong with him? Why couldn't he find a shred of peace in his soul? He'd come through an avalanche, for God's sake. He was alive. Beyond grateful. The thing was, what was he supposed to do with that gratitude? Wrap it around himself never to emerge? Stop free riding? That was the question he'd been trying to run away from for the last two days because every time he tried to answer it, he came up with something different.

Straight after the avalanche, when the snow had stopped thundering and he'd been lying there, blinking up at the sky, all he'd been able to see were the faces of Simone and Yann and Chloe, and all he'd wanted was to be with them, hold them close, never do anything to hurt them. If he'd had to answer the question at that moment, he'd have said without hesitation that he was never venturing onto the mountain again. But when Simone had asked him just hours later, What are you going to do, Dax, going forward? he'd felt a niggling doubt starting, a niggling doubt that had snowballed into full-blown chaos. And he hadn't wanted Simone to see it, so he'd kept his distance, stayed away from her bed, and then he'd felt the pain of hurting her, the pain of feeling responsible for the bruised, worried look in her eyes, and he'd felt torn in two because hurting Simone was the last thing in the world he ever wanted to do.

He didn't want to be feeling like this… Wretched. Guilty. Guilty for still loving the jagged peaks in front of him, guilty because he couldn't stop his eyes searching for lines, guilty because he couldn't seem to switch off that part of himself. He sighed. But how could he switch it off when it was the best part of him, the only part of him that had ever been worth anything? Extreme free riding had given him a place in the world where he could feel safe—ironic!—a place where he knew who he was, what was expected of him. Free riding had given him self-respect, an income of his own, a life he could believe in, but, more than that, it had given him a line to his son, a son who amazed him every day, a son who reminded him so much of himself.

Yann! When Claude had called to tell him, he'd been knocked for a loop. For a moment he'd felt resentful, yes, but then he'd remembered how it had felt, not knowing his own father. He'd felt the pain coming back, the ignominy of not having been conceived in love, of not knowing his father's name, of not even knowing what he looked like. And thinking about all that, he'd felt his heart filling with a million good intentions. He'd gone to collect Yann in love with the idea of being a father, then discovered that he had no idea how to be one. He'd failed over and over again, ached about it every day. And then…then Yann had come down that night and asked about his snowboards…

That had changed everything, set wonderful wheels in motion. Yann loved that he was Dax 'Hasard' D'Aureval, extreme free rider, with over a hundred and seventy thousand followers on social media, sponsors clamouring for his endorsement, and free-riding friends all over the world. He hung on his every word, listened to his every instruction. Yann loved watching his films, ran into his arms now with excited eyes when he came in, wanting to hear about the lines he'd been riding…how fast, how high, how many somersaults. What would Yann think of him if he gave it all up?

He pulled his phone out, scrolling through the pictures. There! He felt his cheeks loosening, warmth filling his chest. Simone had snapped it at the resort that first day he'd been out: Yann's face, rapt. Free riding had made him a hero to his son, but would he still be a hero if he stopped flying down mountains? When Simone had asked him if he was going to tell Yann about the avalanche, he'd had an immediate, visceral reaction: No! He'd hadn't wanted Yann to think he'd messed up, hadn't wanted to risk Yann thinking he was a failure, or that the mountain had beaten him. At that moment he'd felt the full weight of everything pressing down on him. He drew in a slow breath. But the mountain hadn't beaten him! It had tried, but Pierre was right: he'd stayed calm, followed the drill, done everything he was supposed to do, and he'd survived.

He tucked the phone back into his pocket. Riding a snowboard wasn't more important to him than being a father, but it was important because Yann thought it was important. Without it, who would he be, crucially, who would he be to Yann? Would Yann still look at him with admiration, would he still think he was worth listening to, or would he revert to how he'd been before? His heart panged. He couldn't bear the thought of that. Yann gave him so much now and he wanted to give back, wanted to create memories for Yann that he'd never had of his own father. Yann was already excited about the prospect of him conquering Aiguille du Plan. Could he even contemplate letting him down by not doing it?

His heart twisted. But would Simone understand? She could have torn him off a strip over the avalanche, given him the risk lecture, but she hadn't. She'd been kind. Above everything, she was kind. Snow Angel! She'd come to Cham, come to his rescue, opened him up in ways he couldn't believe. She'd said she cared about him, and he was crazy about her. More than crazy! She was making him feel things and think things he'd never felt or thought before. He couldn't stop imagining scenarios, future scenarios, like showing her the mountains from a helicopter in twenty years' time.

Twenty years…

His stomach dipped. But would he get as far as twenty minutes? Oh, God! More than ever, he needed Simone to be kind now, needed her to understand what he had to do and why he had to do it. He'd never asked anyone to be there for him before. He'd never allowed himself to get close to a woman, or to ask anything of a woman, because Colette had stolen his faith. But somehow, miraculously, Simone had kindled it back to life, opened him up to all kinds of possibilities. He had faith in her. Would she come through for him?

'Here you go!' Dax was handing her a beer. His other hand was empty.

'Aren't you having anything?' She was trying to sound casual, but she was feeling anything but. Dax seemed tense. He'd been jolly enough with the kids at bedtime, reading the story, doing the voices, his eyes twinkling, but now he was looking strained. If he hadn't been on the go so much, if he'd actually spent any time with her alone over the past two days, she'd have checked in with him, asked him if he was all right, but that hadn't happened. Last night, he'd crashed on the sofa again after another swimming marathon. She'd tried hard not to get sensitive about it, had tried to rationalise that he was still dealing with the avalanche stuff, but it had stung all the same. Now at least they were in the same room, alone, and awake.

He shook his head. 'No. I'm not drinking to-night…' He dropped down onto the opposite sofa, but he didn't settle back. He was pressing his palms together, taking a deep breath that she could almost feel fluttering in her own belly. His eyes came to hers. 'Simone, I need to talk to you about something…' His gaze was serious, a dark light inside it that she didn't recognise.

'Okay.' She felt a tingling dread winding round her veins. She folded the beer bottle into her arms, feeling its seeping chill. 'What is it?'

He blinked. 'I want to try for Aiguille du Plan… Tomorrow.'

Her lungs emptied. She looked down, seeing spots. It couldn't be true. *No!* He'd told her it was off! She set the bottle down shakily, snatching a breath, and then she looked up. 'I'm sorry…' She swallowed hard. 'Did you just say—?'

'Yes.' His eyes gripped hers. 'It's something I need to do.'

'*Need* to do!' Her heart panged, sparking anger. 'Why? Isn't it enough that you almost died two days ago? You want to, what…have another go? Do it better next time?'

His eyes went loud. 'Of course not.' He leaned forwards, forearms resting on his thighs. 'I'm not trying to kill myself. I'm trying to get some-thing back.'

'What? Your sixth sense?' His face blanched.

Guilt curled in her belly. It had been a low blow, but desperation was twisting her out of shape.

'No! That's still intact.'

'Really?' She could feel her pulse beating through her skin. 'So I can still believe in it—' she swallowed a sharp, dry edge on her tongue '—can I, Dax? Is it going to keep you safe this time?'

'What happened three days ago had nothing to do with…' He sighed, light shifting through his gaze. 'I made mistakes… There was a hold-up with the drone. I lost my focus.'

'And that won't happen again?'

His gaze tightened. 'I won't let it.'

She thought of Gabriel Guillot, Claude Deuzlier, André, and felt a fresh hot lick of anger. 'It's not all down to you. You can't see everything coming, can't control everything, no matter what you think. There's always going to be that one time.' Suddenly she was at a loss. 'What is it, Dax? What the hell is *so* important to you that you're prepared to risk your life again?'

The corners of his mouth tightened. 'My self-respect.'

'Self-respect?' She felt her own mouth tightening. 'Are you sure it isn't ego?' Something flashed behind his eyes. 'Maybe you just can't stand that the mountain almost got the better of you. Are you trying to show the mountain who's boss?' She felt her frustration ramping. 'Is it a man thing? Because I don't get it! You won't win, Dax. Can't you see that? In the end you won't win.' She swallowed hard. 'In case you'd forgotten, you have a son!'

He blinked and then a fierce light came into his eyes. 'He's the *reason* I need to get my self-respect back! Yann *loves* what I do…' He was pulling out his phone, tapping and scrolling, then he was thrusting his hand out, showing her the picture she'd taken herself. 'See this! Yann watching me. You took it! To show me how well I was doing with Yann, to show me how much he respects me.' He lowered the phone, looking at the screen, its light ghosting on his face, picking up a glaze in his eyes. 'He didn't respect me before. He didn't even give me the time of day, no matter what I did. But now, because of what I do, he thinks I'm a hero, and I like it. I want to live up to his expectations. I want to be someone who doesn't give up because of a setback.' His eyes came back to hers, moist and full. 'Snowboarding opened his eyes to me. It's given us a bond, given me the chance to be the father I want to be. Can't you see that? If I stop doing what I do, what happens to all that? What will he think?'

'He'll think you're putting him first. He'll know that he's more important to you than anything else. And if you're alive, and around, then you'll find other things you can bond over. Snowboarding is only the beginning...' She licked her lips. 'And no one's asking you to give it up. Only the high-risk stuff—'

'But that's what I do. It's who I am.' His eyes were filling. 'It's *all* I am, Simone. If I don't get back out there, delivering what I've promised to deliver, then I lose everything.'

'You won't lose me, Dax. Don't I count?' She felt tears burning behind her eyes. 'And Dax D'Aureval, extreme free rider, isn't all you are. You're so much more than that...' Suddenly, the distance between them was getting in the way. She went to sit by him. 'Dax, can't you see? I'm in love with you...' Something warm and intense came into his eyes, turning her inside out. Was opening her heart to him going to make him think again? She felt hope rising. She touched his cheek, flattening her palm against it. 'I love you, so much... I love you for your kindness, and your boundless energy, and for how funny you can be, and because you make me feel protected and safe. You'll notice that none of those things depend on how good you are on a snowboard... I don't want to lose you, Dax. *You!*' She loaded her gaze with everything she could. 'I care about *you.*'

'Oh, Simone.' His eyes were moist again, a

moving tapestry of light and shade. 'If you love me, if you really care about me, then please… support me in this. Understand why I *have* to do it. Please…'

Her heart collapsed. Nothing she was saying was making the slightest bit of difference. She felt tears breaking free, sliding down her cheeks. She wasn't enough. She didn't matter enough. Chloe didn't matter enough, Chloe, who would cry a million oceans if anything happened to him. That momentary fire in his eyes hadn't sparked a declaration of his own, even though she thought she'd seen love flowing through his gaze so many times.

He didn't love her.

She looked down, felt his hand settling on her shoulder. 'Don't cry, Simone. Please. I'll be fine. I don't want you to worry about me.'

She squeezed her eyes shut. What had she done? Fallen for a man so blind to her feelings that he actually thought she was crying because she was worried about him? She *was* worried, but why couldn't he see that she wanted something back from him? If he couldn't see it in her, then his feelings for her were nothing like hers for him. In the woods that day he'd said that what they were doing wasn't a mistake, but it was beginning to feel like one!

She took a breath, wiping her cheeks. If Dax

didn't love her, if her love for him wasn't enough to make him change his mind, then she had to try saving him for Yann's sake. She met his gaze. 'I can't support you. I think you're making a big mistake.' She bit her lips hard, heart tearing. 'I'm washing my hands of you, Dax!'

'No, Simone, please…' The light in his eyes was draining fast. 'Don't say that. I *need* you.'

'No, you don't.' She pushed his hand off her shoulder and picked her phone up off the low table. Was she really going to do this, hit him with the truth about his father? Her fingers were trembling, her pulse was hammering in her ears, but shock and awe was all she had left. She scrolled through the pictures to *that* picture, then turned the phone around so he could see. 'What you *need* is to see this!'

His eyes flicked to the screen, locking on, then narrowing, his mouth falling open. 'What's this?'

'It's your father. Gabriel Dax Guillot.' She felt fresh tears burning behind her eyes. 'He died in an avalanche on Mont Blanc before you were born.'

'I don't understand…' Bruised eyes gripped hers. 'How did you…? Where did you get it?'

'Photo exhibition at the Alpine Museum. I thought it was you, and then I realised…' She swallowed hard. 'You need to think about it,

Dax.' He looked dazed, shell-shocked. She felt her throat filling with tears, her heart breaking for him, for herself. Suddenly she couldn't bear to look at him. She got to her feet, speaking to the floor. 'You've paid me to be here, I know, but if you ride that line tomorrow, then Chloe and I are leaving—'

'On Christmas Eve?' He was getting to his feet. 'You can't. Please, don't go.'

'I'm sorry, Dax. It's just something I have to do.' She took a backwards step, blinking back tears, dying inside. 'You of all people should understand!'

CHAPTER FOURTEEN

Christmas Eve...

HE DIALLED PIERRE'S number then pressed the phone to his ear, lifting his gaze. The mountains beyond the cemetery wall were rose-pink, turning gold as the first rays of the rising sun broke around their contours.

New day...

'Dax!' Pierre sounded primed and ready for action. 'What's up?'

He felt a small pang of not-quite-guilt. 'I'm not coming, Pierre. I'm sorry if you're packed already—'

'Are you okay?'

'Yes.' He flicked a glance at the headstone in front of him. 'I'm absolutely fine, but I can't ride that line... I'm postponing indefinitely.'

There was a long silence, then Pierre sighed. 'I can't believe I'm saying this, but I'm glad. To be honest, I was surprised when you said it was a go for today... I think that avalanche really shook you up.'

Not only the avalanche.

'It did. I need to think about Yann.'

'I get that, man. If I had kids, I'd be rethinking too.'

He took a breath. 'So I'll catch you after Christmas, then?'

'Absolutely!' Pierre's voice filled with a smile. 'Have a good one, Dax.'

'You, too.' He tapped his teeth together. Would he have a good Christmas? Maybe, if he could straighten himself out. He pocketed the phone and looked down at the headstone.

In Loving Memory
Gabriel Dax Guillot

He felt a lump thickening in his throat. At least they'd found the body. At least his *papa* had had a proper burial. A shiver hovered between his shoulder blades. So many avalanche victims were never found. Christ! The thought of never being found...of being buried alive, no air to breathe. The thought of never seeing Yann again, or Simone, or Chloe... He screwed his eyes shut, feeling a burn prickling behind them. What had he been thinking? What bug in his brain had convinced him that attempting to ride Aiguille du Plan was a good idea when it was, patently, the worst idea he'd ever had?

He pushed his hands through his hair. The bug that had always been there, of course. Insecurity about who he was, where he fitted, what he was for. He was a walking identity crisis! Free riding had fixed it for over a decade, but then Claude had called, and it had kicked off all over again. What was he...a father or an extreme free rider? He'd wanted to be both, and Yann's interest in snowboarding had made it seem possible. But the avalanche had kicked him back again, and for some reason, to his panicked, bent-out-of-shape brain, Aiguille du Plan had seemed like a solution, but it wasn't. He knew that now for sure. The only way he could solve his identity crisis was by choosing a side, the right side. He had to accept fully and finally that he was a father first.

A family man!

He drew in a breath, letting it settle. It sounded fine, more than fine. He felt a smile coming. But of course it did! Hadn't he felt the whole 'family man' vibe pulsing through him from the moment they'd set off for Chamonix? Rescuing Maurice! That ridiculously happy feeling he'd had concocting the whole magic Christmas tree thing...the sheer joy he'd felt seeing their faces when they'd come in...and that glow he'd felt inside showing Simone and the kids around, showing off the home he loved, that feeling of wanting them to love it too. Walking around with his phone all afternoon because he hadn't wanted to miss a second with them, not a single second...

He dropped down, running his eyes over the headstone. And it was all because Yann had started engaging with him in the car. After months of nothing, getting something back from his son had boosted him into the stratosphere, had ramped up his paternal instincts to the max, made every second feel all the more precious. He closed his eyes. And yes, if he followed that line, he could see that it had felt like that because he'd never had a single second with his own father. He'd learned to live with the pain, but it had always been there deep down, the gaping chasm in his soul. And now he was here, with his *papa* at last, closer than he'd ever been and it was too late. Too damn late! Dust! Bones! Nothing to have, nothing to hold. He felt his eyes burning again and squeezed them shut. *Crazy!* Even now he was trying to hold it in instead of letting it out. He pressed his palms to his eyes, felt a sob filling his throat.

Let it out!

The blinding shock of that photograph, spending all night searching on his computer, finding two living grandparents in Argentière, finding out that Gabriel could ski before he could walk, finding out where Gabriel was buried, that it wasn't so far away... He gulped a ragged breath, steadying himself, wiping his eyes. Shock after shock after shock. But there was a kind of peace too, trickling in. Knowing his context, knowing who he took after, not just looks-wise, but with that sense for the mountain—not the whole sixth-sense thing, which was sounding pretty arrogant to him in his head now, but that sense of belonging, that whole running-in-the-blood thing that seemed to run through Yann too.

He drew in a breath, rising to his feet. Had Gabriel known that Colette was pregnant when he'd gone off with Deuzlier's team that day? Had he stopped, even for a second, to consider the possible consequences? And could Dax really blame him if he hadn't? If Simone hadn't brought him to his senses by showing him the picture, then maybe he'd have been climbing a cliff right now.

He shuddered. Actions. Consequences. He wanted to talk to Colette. Was the way she'd been with him down to Gabriel? Had she loved his *papa* fiercely, never got over losing him? Had she seen Gabriel in him all the time and hadn't been able to cope with her emotions? Was losing Gabriel the reason she hated

Chamonix, the reason why she never visited? So many questions… Maybe he could use Gabriel to open a door with Colette, find a new beginning somehow…

He inhaled deeply. Perhaps it was wishful thinking, but daring to hope was fine because he was feeling stronger now, more centered, more in control. If it weren't for Simone seeing that picture, he'd never have known all this, would never have been in this place, reassessing everything. If it weren't for Simone…

Simone!

He closed his eyes for a beat. That first moment, snowflakes in her hair, snowflakes on her cheeks… That smile. Stealing his breath, stopping his heart…his heart. *Yes!* Last night, she'd said she was in love with him. She'd put her heart on the line trying to stop him doing a stupid thing. She'd said, *No.* No one had ever said no to him before, but she'd said it because she loved him. And he'd been so lost inside his own head and his own stupid crisis that he'd tried to use it to lever her support instead of telling her…telling her that he was in love with her too. He felt warmth pulsing in his chest, a strong pulsing warmth growing stronger, streaming through his veins. *Yes!* That had to be it. *Love!* Why else would he have kept picturing her in his future? Twenty years in… Why else would she have been his first thought after the avalanche? He'd wanted to run to her with all his heart, the way he wanted to run to her now… If that wasn't love, then what was?

Simone tugged the beanie down around her ears and set off walking. There was only one way to go if she wanted to step out, and that was down the twisting private road that led away from the house. Dax always kept it clear and gritted so it was a better option than trudging through the snow on the slopes, slipping and stumbling. Her insides were stumbling around all over the place as it was, churning away.

She'd heard Dax leaving, the throaty rumble of his four-by-four sliding out of the garage before daybreak. She hadn't been sleeping anyway, but after that, she'd been wide awake, twisting like a fish on a line. As soon as Chantal had arrived, she'd slipped out. She couldn't face breakfast, couldn't face telling Yann and Chloe in a fake cheery voice that Dax was on the mountain. Her stomach clenched. On the mountain. Or falling off it. Or being swallowed by an avalanche…

She felt tears prickling at the edges of her eyes. What was *wrong* with him? How *could* he have gone to ride that line after seeing what had happened to his father, the father he'd missed, the father he wished he'd known, the father he'd wished had been around to offset his unfathomable mother? Gabriel's absence had impacted his life in so many ways, and he knew it, *knew it!* That photograph had been her last card. She'd thought it would bring him to his senses but he'd gone off that morning all the same.

Was it really for Yann, so that Yann would see him as a hero? Did he really believe that Yann would think less of him if he stopped doing the extreme stuff? It was so great the way the two of them had bonded. It was what she'd wanted more than anything but connecting over a love of snowboarding had backfired spectacularly! Now it seemed to have become the wind beneath Dax's wings. She'd tried to tell him that snowboarding was only the start, that they'd find other interests, other ways to connect. She'd tried telling him that he was so much more than a free rider but it hadn't worked. And now she was trapped. *Knowing* that he was out there taking massive, massive risks, *knowing* that something catastrophic could happen. Feeling heartsick and sick to the stomach.

She swallowed hard. Telling Dax she was washing her hands of him was one thing, but actually doing it was another. She couldn't switch off the anxiety that was clawing at her belly any more than she could switch off the love inside, the love she'd thought, for one tantalising instant, was going to turn him around. His gaze had filled with such a warm, wonderful, burning light, that she'd thought she was winning, but then he'd harnessed her declaration and twisted it to his own ends.

'If you love me, if you really care about me, then please...support me in this. Understand why I have to do it. Please...'

She kicked a stone, sending it scuttling across the road. Understanding wasn't the issue. She got him, got that his sport had given him a place in the world where he felt good about himself. She got what a boost to him it was that in Yann's eyes he'd gone from zero to hero. She could see the line of his thinking as clearly as he saw lines in the mountains, but just because it was a clear line, it didn't mean it was the right one. He needed to be a father first, needed to believe that he could still be a hero to Yann without pulling off the extreme stunts that could land him in an early grave. When she'd snapped that picture of Yann, Dax had been *at the resort*, a safe place where he'd still managed to blow all of their minds. Couldn't he see that flying down the resort slopes, turning tricks, was mesmerising enough? It was for her. Last night, she'd told him that all the things she loved about him had nothing to do with his snowboard, but it wasn't true. On his board, Dax was a firework, a rocket! She loved seeing him soar, and spin, throwing himself upside down, seeing all that hard, bright energy he had. It absolutely *was* one of the things she loved about him.

Love...

She felt her heart twisting, tears thickening in her throat. Dax had made her *feel* again but loving him was too hard. How could she love him on his terms? And the thought of Chloe getting even a millimetre closer to him, of herself getting even a millimetre—

Her breath stopped.

Was that his car coming up the hill? She stared, heart banging, legs suddenly shaking. *Yes!* Definitely his. But how? The climb to the head of the couloir was a good three hours. It was too soon for him to be back, unless... She felt tears prickling again. Unless he'd turned back...

The car was slewing to a halt, grit flying, and then Dax was tumbling out, running up, his eyes full of feverish light. 'I didn't go, Sim!' His hands were on her shoulders, his breath coming out in little billows. 'I'm not going, ever. It's one hundred per cent off!'

She swallowed hard, feeling anger and relief fighting for space in her heart. 'And you were going to tell me when...?' Tears were welling up, making it hard to speak. 'You went off... I thought you were...' A sob was rising, filling her throat. 'I can't do this, caring about you, loving you...' His eyes were glistening, tearing her heart out. She swallowed hard again. 'Have you any idea how worried I've been?'

'I'm sorry.' He was blinking. 'I should have left a note, or texted. I was so deep in my own head, I didn't think...' His gaze tightened on hers. 'But I'm going to change, Sim. I'm going to be better at this relationship stuff.'

Relationship stuff? Did he think they were still in a relationship? She felt a small spark igniting inside, a flutter starting somewhere. She took a breath, noticing his clothes, regular clothes, not climbing gear. She felt a frown coming. 'So, where have you been...?'

'Argentière...' A shadow crossed his face. 'To visit my father's grave... To pay my respects.'

Her heart twisted. 'Oh, Dax...' She blinked, felt tears trickling down her cheeks. 'I'm so sorry about Gabriel. I never even said that last night and I should have! I'm so, so sorry.'

'It's all right. You had other things on your mind, like trying to talk some sense into me...' A soft light came into his eyes. 'But there's definitely something I should have said to you last night...' He was cupping her face, his hands all warm, and then his gaze turned so deep and full that it was hard to keep breathing. 'I love you and, in case you think that's not enough, it comes with a promise…' She felt her heart melting, the fluttering moving upwards in waves. 'No more risks, even if Yann thinks I'm lame. I can do other things with snowboarding…safe things… I've already got some ideas…' He took a breath. 'But the main thing is I know what I want now.' A smile touched his lips. 'It's you, Simone, and the kids… I want us to be a family, want it with all my heart. Just don't leave me…' His voice was cracking. 'Please, don't wash your hands of me.' His eyes were burning into hers, turning her inside out. 'I'll do whatever it takes.'

He meant it. She could feel it all the way to her bones, could feel happiness, love, and hope lifting her up, higher and higher, and suddenly it was impossible not to put her arms around his neck, impossible not to slide her fingers into his supremely touchable hair. 'Even move mountains?'

He broke into the smile that undid her every time. 'Now that happens to be my very particular skill…' And then she was being folded into his arms, and his lips were on hers, and the ground was sliding away, but she didn't mind in the slightest because it really was the best kind of dizzy.

EPILOGUE

Chamonix, one year later...

SIMONE WENT CLOSER to the front. The red *D'Aureval Snowboard School* banners looked great behind the small stage, but the stage was maddeningly empty. Where was Dax? And where were the kids?

Had Felix slipped his collar again? Maybe they had all gone after him, but *no*, Dax wouldn't bother himself with the puppy this close to his grand opening ceremony. She turned, searching the crowd. Maybe he was caught up with someone, signalling desperately for her to rescue him. She scanned the rows. He wasn't with Gabriel's parents, his grandparents. They were sitting in the front row, wrapped up well against the cold, their faces glowing with pride.

Warmth filled her chest. They'd been overjoyed when Dax had contacted them. They had welcomed him into their lives with open arms, told him all about his *papa*, even had their photographs of Gabriel copied for him. And they were delighted with Yann, their great-grandson!

She shifted her gaze, sliding her eyes over the groups of chattering guests. Friends, snowboarding buddies, and reps from the companies that were still sponsoring Dax to make instructional videos and safety videos, featuring their kit, of course! She held in a smile. He'd thought they'd drop him, but his face and name still had currency, even though he wasn't doing the extreme stuff any more. She bit her lips together. It was a pity that Colette hadn't come, but they hadn't really expected her to. Dax was making slow progress there, but at least Colette was beginning to open up about Gabriel. Baby steps.

She caught Pierre's eye. He winked, gave the camera a little jiggle. All set! Dax had asked Pierre to shoot some stuff to promote the school on social media, not that he needed any promotion. Being taught to free ride by Dax 'Hasard' D'Aureval was a massive draw.

Suddenly the microphone blared. 'Hello…'

She spun round, heart pulsing. Dax was on the stage after all, bang on time, and looking as gorgeous as ever! He must have slipped past her.

She threw him a smile, which he threw right back with a cheeky wink.

He leaned into the microphone. 'Thanks for

coming out on Christmas Eve, everyone!' He broke into a smile. 'It's a big day...' There was an appreciative murmur from the crowd. His hand went up to his head, fingers raking through his hair. She felt a fluttering in her stomach. He did that when he was nervous, not that anyone else would know. He was squaring himself up to the microphone, still smiling. 'I almost can't believe that today I'm opening my own free-riding school, but I am, and it's all because a year ago I promised a very special person that I was going to stop riding risky lines.'

She felt her heart filling, a tear wanting to slip out.

'I loved riding those lines, I'll admit, but you should know that I've had no trouble keeping that promise because somehow, miraculously, I've been blessed with a family and...' his voice was cracking a little '...and being there for them, and with them, is more important to me than a thirty-second thrill.' His eyes came to hers, full and intense. 'Why go for thirty seconds when you can have a lifetime?' She bit her lips together, feeling tears welling behind her eyes. 'Simone...' He was holding out his hand, such a look in his eyes. 'Would you join me up here, please?'

Her heart panged. What was he doing? This wasn't the speech he'd shown her. She swallowed hard and went up, feeling a blush tingling madly in her cheeks.

'And Yann, Chloe and, last but not least, Felix the disaster dog, will you also come up here, please?'

There was a movement at the front. So that was where the kids had been! Standing with Victor. Or, hiding behind Victor… They had funny little smirks on their faces, and they were looking at Dax, avoiding her gaze. She felt a brow furrowing. What was going on?

He was leaning into the microphone again, but he was looking directly at her. 'As I was saying, why go for a thirty-second thrill when, if you play your cards right, you could enjoy a thrill that lasts for ever?' A smile touched his lips. 'That's the thrill I'm after, so, Simone…'

No…

His gaze tightened on hers. 'You are the light of my life, the light of our kids' lives, and you're also Felix's favourite human, so, I think we're all agreed…'

Chloe and Yann were chuckling, meeting her eye now, except that she couldn't see very well because her eyes were all wet.

'Simone…' He was coming forwards, dropping down to his knees, his eyes burning into hers. 'Will you please, please, marry me?'

Her heart exploded softly. Only Dax could

have come up with this, proposing in front of everyone, or, if Chloe's and Yann's faces were anything to go by, maybe they'd conspired. Yes! Definitely, they had. She felt a smile wobbling onto her lips, tears sliding down her cheeks. But it was perfect, because they were a family. She took a breath, fastening her eyes on his, feeling his love flowing back. 'Yes! I will…with all my heart.'

'Sick!' He was laughing, his eyes brimming too, and then he was turning to Yann and Chloe. 'Kids…*now* would be a good time…'

They bumbled forward, Felix straining on his lead with Yann hanging on for dear life, Chloe rooting in her pocket, giggling, then handing Dax a small box.

Dax popped it open, revealing a twinkling diamond, his eyes holding hers, full of smiles. 'In my head this was so much slicker.'

She couldn't stop laughing and crying. 'It's perfect.' He was sliding the ring onto her finger, and then he was on his feet, kissing her, laughing into her mouth, and the crowd were clapping and whistling, and Felix was barking, and all she could think was that it was the most perfect moment ever, the most perfect Christmas proposal.

* * * * *

*If you enjoyed this story, check out these
other great reads from
Ella Hayes*

Tycoon's Unexpected Caribbean Fling
Unlocking the Tycoon's Heart
Italian Summer with the Single Dad
Her Brooding Scottish Heir

All available now!